JASON MARINKO'S
STARRY NIGHTMARES

EVERY NIGHT IS NOT STARRY,
EVERY NIGHTMARE IS NOT JUST A DREAM

Charleston, SC
www.PalmettoPublishing.com

Starry Nightmares

First Edition

Paperback ISBN: 978-1-7369508-1-4

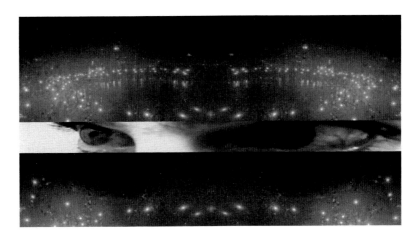

FOR THOSE WHO HAD TO BURN IN ORDER
TO FEEL THE MOONLIGHT SHINE

Timetheavenger.com

CONTENTS

THE WRITER'S ROLE IS TO MENACE
THE PUBLIC'S CONSCIENCE.

—Rod Serling to the Library of Congress, 1968

WHY DON'T YOU GO OUTSIDE?

The governor declared a state of emergency due to the storm, and that was just fine by Andrew and his friends. School was closed and the guys came over to spend the day playing the new game, *Gridiron Greats Football*. Usually, they played the game at Donnie's house but couldn't that day. Donnie's parents had to open the bakery they owned, leaving no adults home. Christian's sister was home and claimed the house for herself while their dad was away on business and Mark's house was off-limits because the uncle he lived with was a hoarder whose home had been cited on multiple occasions by the board of health.

Each of the boys selected a team to manage for the season. They often played against the computer, which offered little competition.

The real fun began when their selected teams met in the schedule or in the playoffs. Andrew was finishing up his game against the Brisbane Bloodhounds, and Donnie and Mark were slated to go head-to-head next. The trash talk had already begun and soon escalated into a wrestling match.

The sounds of Mark screaming to be released from Donnie's headlock in the corner of Andrew's room broke Martin's concentration. Andrew's dad told the boys to keep it down twice before because he was using the day off to file his taxes online. Jumping up from his desk in anger, he went to Andrew's room and flung the door open. They were lounging around, eating junk food, and, if he didn't know better, he swore he saw Donnie and Mark dry humping each other in the corner by his son's bed.

"What the hell are you guys doing in here?!" Martin screamed at the top of his lungs, causing Andrew to drop his controller in fear.

"Nothing, Dad. We're just playing video games and hanging out. Why?" Andrew asked, responding meekly and embarrassed.

"Can't you guys go to Donnie's?"

"My parents opened the bakery today, Mister Nelson. There's no one home."

Having spent the entire morning and afternoon working on his taxes, Martin decided his son and his friends needed to learn the value of a dollar.

"Why don't you guys go outside?"

"And do what, Dad?"

"All you do is sit around and play that game like babies. When I was your age, Andy, I had a girlfriend and a job. You don't lift a finger except to play that damn game station or whatever it is."

Speaking from his own experience, Martin recalled the prospect of earning money was always a motivating factor for him in his youth and decided to offer some encouragement.

"Tell you what, Andy, you guys go out to the garage, take some shovels, and clear a path to the driveway and the front walk, and I'll give you twenty dollars each."

Unable to contain himself, Donnie laughed at the prospect of earning such a minuscule amount of money for labor he saw as ridiculous. Mark, on the other hand, was already putting his jacket on, while Christian and Andrew slowly got up from the floor. Seeing reluctance in the boys' body language, Martin decided to sweeten the deal and get them out of the house longer than a half hour.

"After you're done with our house, you guys can go door-to-door in the neighborhood shoveling people's walks for cash. On top of that, I'll match whatever you guys make shoveling, dollar for dollar. What do you say?"

"That's not a bad deal," Donnie said, his mood altered by the bonus offered. Andrew turned off his system and the television and was the last of his friends outside. Martin returned to his taxes, feeling he'd provided the kids some much-needed initiative. He looked at the clear path from his door and saw the kids finishing up the walk for the widow across the street.

Donnie elected himself treasurer of their excursion. By his estimates, they needed to expand the territory they were shoveling in to make any real money. They got fifteen dollars from the widow and only another ten from the couple at the end of Andy's street. They knocked on the door of every walk not shoveled, splitting up to cover more houses.

"Hardly anyone has cash on them anymore," Christian said in frustration.

"I know. Half the houses on my street said they'd pay us but hadn't been to the bank yet," Andrew agreed as the four of them walked to the next block over. A grown man passed them with a shovel balanced over his shoulder, wearing a ski mask and hood. The boys giggled as they passed, and then Donnie threw a poorly packed snowball at Andrew's back.

"Hey, that guy must be friends with your dad, Andy." Donnie teased, getting out of the way of the snowball hurled back at him by Andrew. The boys engaged in a brief snowball fight until Christian put them back on task.

"There's probably more people like that guy out here with the same idea. We got to hurry up if we want to make more than twenty-five dollars," Christian yelled, bringing the horseplay to a stop.

"Fifty dollars. Remember, Mister Nelson is doubling what we make. Hey, does that count for the eighty bucks he's already paying us for your house?" Donnie asked.

"I doubt it," Andrew said, irritated by the snow inside his gloves.

The next block over was less lucrative than Andrew's street. Just one house in the middle of the street asked them to shovel, and when they were done, the young girl living there wanted to pay them through her online account. Since they were rushed out of Andy's room by his father, Donnie and Christian left their phones plugged into the outlet, charging. Mark didn't own a cell phone and Andy only had a savings account that his parents took care of.

April Washington deposited all her tip money in her bank's ATM, after dancing until closing at Divine Angels. She looked upon the wide-eyed teens that woke her by banging on her door. Donnie nudged Mark's arm in response to April's rock-hard nipples visible through her midnight blue sateen robe toughened by the cold air.

"I'm so sorry. I forgot I hit the bank after work last night, boys. You want to come back tomorrow or something?"

"That's fine." Christian replied.

"No problem." Mark agreed.

"Yeah, we can come back," Donnie said eagerly anticipating getting an eyeful of April a second time. Mark rosy, red cheeks turned another shade of red as all he could do was nod in approval.

"Wait, no! I can write you guys a check," April said, striding away from the doorway to get her purse. Her robe glided with her as she walked away, revealing a side profile of her killer body and just a midnight blue sateen matching bra and panties under the robe.

"Holy crap! That chick is smoking hot," Donnie said, unable to contain his excitement.

"You see those tits? I'm in love," he continued.

"Shut up. She's coming back," Andrew said.

"Okay here's a check for forty and here take this. It'll just make me fat," April said smiling with the check pinned by her thumb through the screen door atop a heart-shaped box of Valentine's Day candy.

"Thank you," all the boys responded in unison.

"Wait a second," April called out, causing them to turn from stepping off the porch.

"Something for the inconvenience," she said with a playful grin with her head peeking out the screen door. The boys stood in awe as she backed away, closed the screen door, opened up her robe, and pulled down the top of her bra. She revealed her amazing breasts through the glass door and gave a slight shimmy before closing her robe, holding her index finger over her lips to signify silence and waving goodbye.

"This is the greatest day of my life!" Andrew exclaimed as April cackled to herself, hearing his proclamation through the walls of her house.

The sight of April's bare breasts inspired them, the forty-dollar check boosted their profits, and, while they were wet, Cold, and a bit tired, they pressed on farther from Andrew's house.

Martin Nelson clicked the submit button and breathed a sigh of relief. He finished his state taxes and was starving, so he made himself a sandwich. Looking at the clock on the stove, he noticed the boys had been gone for two hours. With them out so long he initially worried, and then laughed at the thought of having to fork over his two-hundred-dollar state return to his son and his goofy friends.

The kids didn't get another customer for five more blocks and were considering heading back when Mark got an idea.

5

"No one ever shovels the sidewalks by my uncle's house and people have cash around there all the time."

The boy's observations, while naïve, were not inaccurate. His uncle's home bordered the township and the city. Homes were often unattended due to being vacant; some were just neglected by their owners. The cash he spoke of was from hand-to-hand drug transactions he witnessed from his front porch. Mark was the quietest of the group and only spoke up when he had a good idea or a worthwhile contribution.

"You guys really want to walk all the way down to Haventon Court?" Andrew asked.

"It's like only five more blocks from where we already are," Donnie said, considering the distance they had already traveled.

"If we get enough, maybe Mark can buy a system and we can play each other online instead of having to wait all the time," Christian said.

So, toward Mark's they went as the snow stopped falling and cars began to crowd the road. Andrew was cold and tired. Though his friends slept in that morning, his mom insisted he wake up and clean his room before they came over. He didn't want to go inside Mark's house to warm up. He was seeking a diversion, any diversion, to head back to his own house.

Two blocks away from Mark's street, Andrew conjured up an idea. He saw a house with the light on and a snow-covered car in the small driveway.

"Guys, look! I know the people who live in that house. My dad always says they have a lot of money. Let's just do this one and head back, because if my dad orders takeout, he won't have cash on him to pay us today, and we'll have to wait."

"Who lives there?" Donnie asked, suspicious, but interested in his friend's idea.

"I don't know, but they need shoveling done and they'll probably pay us," Andrew replied, as the tone from his cell phone went off.

"Okay come right home after that house," Martin Nelson instructed his son before hanging up. The other three boys were already on the porch talking to a man through a partially opened screen door when Andrew ended the call from his father and hurried to join them.

"He said just do the front and not to worry about the driveway. You sure this guy is rich? He kind of looked like a bum," Donnie asked Andrew as he slammed the shovel into the pile of snow at the bottom of the steps.

"His house smelled like a combination of mothballs and puke," Christian added. His observation was overheard by the homeowner Kenneth Chalmers as Christian's voice carried up the porch and through the bay window. Behind the curtain, Chalmers observed the boys outside his front window. The sound of boots stomping up his wooden steps made him jump up from his recliner in fear.

The last time he heard a barrage of boots stomping up to his door was when the police came to a different house to apprehend him fifteen years ago. He was released from the penitentiary a year ago and was able to move into this house six months later. A program set up by the county for first-time offenders worked out in his favor. Chalmers was required to sign up for the registered offenders list but did not because he was planning on hanging himself anyway. He figured the knock at his door was authorities citing him for his failing to register. His concern turned to excitement at the sight of the four boys outside.

His dentures moved around in his mouth as he grinned. The loss of his real teeth was not natural; they were something he left behind in prison once the cause of his incarceration was discovered by the other inmates. Inside the walls of the penitentiary Ken Chalmers became the recipient of something the incarcerated refer to as "prison justice," a treatment reserved for those considered the absolute worst living among them.

The sight of the kids with the rosy, red cheeks outside excited him and he didn't even realize he was touching himself standing in the window. He ran his free hand up and down the ribbing of his undershirt, overcome with desire. The mop wringer bludgeoning that left him near dead and toothless in jail was but a distant memory. His lower lip quivered and his pulse pounded in his throat.

The tea kettle whistled on his stove, snapping Ken Chalmers out of his trance and giving him a twisted idea at the same time. Once finished, the kids stomped up the steps again and banged on the door.

"Come on in. Warm up while I get the money for you," he said holding the door open for the kids, who were eager to accept his invitation. Daylight had departed and they were all cold. Andrew could hardly feel his fingers. Dropping the shovels onto the porch, they headed into Chalmers's house single file.

"Just take your boots off first, don't want to get the carpet soaked. I have to run upstairs, that's where all my money is. Help yourselves to something warm to drink in the kitchen. I've got warm cider, tea, and hot chocolate I made to thank you kids for helping me out." Andrew decided Christian's estimate of the scent of mothballs was accurate, but there was not a trace of puke. The scent of cider and hot chocolate made the house smell more like Christmas, mothball and Christmas.

"If he's going to his stash, he's probably going to pay us a lot," Donnie said, slapping Andrew's shoulder in excitement. Christian was already going for the cider, happy to see the disposable cups left out. He hated drinking from glasses in other people's houses. Mark helped himself to a full Styrofoam cup of hot chocolate and was already heading for a refill. Andrew opened April's Valentine's Day heart, offering the candy to his friends to enjoy with their drinks, and then had a cup for himself.

Setting the candy box down on the counter, he took a cup for himself. Mark sat at the kitchen table, his face flushed red. Andrew poured the chocolate as Christian removed his hat, feeling overheated as well. Donnie pulled out a third chair from the table and gazed toward the ceiling.

"What the hell is this guy doing taking a dum—" Donnie began to say before his head slammed onto the table causing it to tip over. Donnie lay on the floor unconscious. Christian jumped up at the sight of Donnie's face-first plunge, but then fainted himself. Andrew dropped his cup and ran to aid his friends, as Mark slumped unconsciously, his head hanging backward, still in the chair. The commotion brought Kenneth Chalmers storming down the steps. The sight of his crazed face with a hunting knife and nylon rope in his hands terrified Andrew.

Petrified, Andrew ran to the back door, unzipping his jacket as Chalmers chased behind him. The door refused to budge, even after Andrew untwisted the deadbolt still held tight.

"Come 'ere, you pink little piggy!" Chalmers screamed. With saliva bubbling through his gritted teeth, he hurdled over Donnie's unconscious body toward Andy who was trembling while fumbling with the lock screen on his phone. Chalmers's right foot planted atop the box of Valentine's Day candy knocked to the floor by the tipped over table. The box gave way, sliding on the linoleum floor, and sent Chalmers toppling over. Andy pressed redial on his phone dialing the Martin's house. Chalmers aimed the knife in the trembling boy's direction. Pinned between the back door and the crazed lunatic, Andy gasped.

Having been incarcerated for the past fifteen years, Kenneth Chalmers was more astute to the effects of knockout drugs, like quaaludes, than he was on technology of the day. Once again, the sound of stomping feet raced up his porch. This time, the front door was kicked in by the police who were able to track Andrew's location from the Find My Phone app on his parent's computer.

Unfortunately for Andrew it was not soon enough. Before his parents and the police were able to track his location, the cellphone fell back into the inside pocket of his unzipped coat. Andrew tried to call for help before Ken Chalmers stabbed him to prevent his escape. When they stormed into Chalmers's residence, they found the other three boys unharmed but traumatized and tied up in the cellar. Chalmers was lifting up the floorboards to hide Andrew's body that was covered in shrink-wrap.

The courts sentenced Chalmers to life imprisonment and the prosecutor vowed to retry him, should the state's death penalty policy be overturned. Donnie, Christian, and Mark stayed friends and even attended the same college together, never forgetting Andrew, the friend they lost. Mark was never able to recover from the trauma of that day. He dropped out, became reclusive, and wound up homeless once his uncle was evicted.

Donnie arrived at the service in his Middleton PD uniform and sat beside Christian whose tie and collar were distressed from dressing in a hurry following surgery. Mark's funeral was the first time Donnie and Christian saw Martin Nelson since the Chalmers trial. He appeared aged well beyond his years. Walking past the two young men he attempted to speak, but only managed a nod, followed by an attempted smile that was neutralized by his permanent frown.

After the service Donnie and Christian went out for drinks and reminisced about Mark and Andrew. They spoke to one another for the first time since they were kids about that fateful day that Martin Nelson asked the four friends, "Why don't you go outside?"

Missed By None

On her way home from work, Janet slowed her car down outside Jolene'Z. Turning her head from left to right, she searched for a space that could fit her mammoth of a sedan. She improvised by turning on the hazard lights and double-parking out front. She flung open the door of the corner bar and gave a look of disgust to the smiling kid at the register. Janet didn't like much, but she liked her routine. Jolene'Z at the end of her day was part of that routine. The kid at the counter was not, and neither was the music blasting from the jukebox.

"Good evening. What can I get for you?" asked the boy with white teeth that gleamed in the dark neighborhood bar.

"Where's Mike?" Janet huffed over the vibrating, base blasting song that rattled her skull as she scanned the bar in aggravation.

Most came into Jolene'Z to buy package goods and dash. The only people who took a seat at the bar were regulars or the occasional passerby who wandered in and enjoyed a shot and a beer-type joint. This was the case with the two young ladies Mike was chatting up.

He felt Janet's eyes boring into his back when he turned around and immediately rushed over to the register.

"Hey Janet, how are you hon? This is my sister's kid Gary here, just turned eighteen, so he can give me a hand around here." Mike explained, placing his arm around his nephew with a proud smile.

"Was this place ever busy enough that you needed help Mike?" Janet looked the two girls up and down, suspecting they weren't even twenty-one. They giggled and spun on the barstools to the music eagerly waiting for Mike to resume carrying on with them.

"You mind? I'm double parked," she continued, recalling how she once had a figure similar to the girls at the bar. Mike jumped to attention and placed a bottle in a brown paper bag.

"Anything to chase, Jan?" About to key in Janet's purchase, his question caused her to give him a look of further annoyance.

"This here is a special customer Gary. Been coming in here since I was your age, if you can believe that." Mike tapped the keys of the register as Janet forced loose bills and change into his hand. "And always has exact change. Can't beat that." Mike handed Janet the bottle, which she snatched from him.

"If it's going to take me this long to get what I came for Mike, I'll start going to that new liquor store by my work," Janet said with her back to Mike, who shook his head to Gary as she exited Jolene'Z.

Driving up to the house, Janet's car bumped into the curb. She exited, cursing to herself; her neighbor was pretending to get her mail and eyeing her up. Instantly she wished she didn't take the time to empty out the overflowing metal tray filled with extinguished Pall Mall 100 filters. Janet knew she wasn't looking for mail, she was looking to strike up conversation. The extra time to clean out the car was going to cost her. Janet's shoulders tensed as Ruth's voice bellowed out in her direction.

"Hey Jan! I was going away this weekend. I'm staying at my son's house. Can you look out for a package I'm expecting? John and I are trying new vitamins."

"Not a chance Ruth," Janet replied slamming the car door shut and rushing toward her porch. Ruth's smile turned to a frown. She and John went out of their way to be kind to Janet, who refused to reciprocate. She hated the swarms of alley cats Janet fed in her backyard and dealt with it because she felt sorry for her.

"You know Jan, the whole backyard smells like cat piss! John can't even grow his tomatoes out there because of all those strays on your back porch. You can't even keep an eye out for my package? It's not like you go anywhere, on the weekends anyway. I'm going to tell John to stop taking out your trash and recycling. Lord knows he's bound to get a hernia with all those bottles your recycling bucket is filled with," Ruth exclaimed.

Halfway in the screen door Janet stopped unlocking the deadbolt, then turned to face Ruth standing on the curb near her car. She let the screen door slam and held a finger up to Ruth while clenching the neck of the bottle with her purse and her left hand.

"What is it you want from me Ruth? I'm divorced, my kids won't talk to me, people at my job hate me, and the landlord hates that I feed the cats too, even though it didn't bother him when he still wanted to screw me, but I guess that's why I get charged late fees now. I'm sorry if I don't give a shit about John's garden, your package, your son, or his bucktoothed wife. Now fuck off!" Janet screamed, then slammed the inside door so hard it made Ruth shudder.

It was routine for Janet to change out of her work clothes, then retrieve the trays from the back porch and fill them for the cats' supper. Today she took off her coat, kicked her shoes into a corner, and then went straight into the living room. She didn't even take the bottle out of the paper bag, let alone get a glass from the kitchen. A schoolteacher that looked like her ex was a contestant on *Jeopardy*. It made her happy to see him lose in the final round. She passed out halfway through *Wheel of Fortune* and was woken an hour later by the caterwauling cries of the hungry felines at her back porch.

"Shut the hell up!" Janet screamed from the broken-down, beige sofa her mother bought in 1986, a year before she died. Janet finished off her bottle, covered her ears with the pillow, and then passed out. She didn't need to set an alarm to wake up for work. She went to sleep with the television on and the bubbly, valley girl voice of the morning show host had her feeling like crawling out of her skin.

Clicking off the television as fast as possible she groaned, then proceeded to hurdle scattered Home Shopping Network boxes that covered the stairwell. She turned on the CD player that had disc two of *The Carpenters Ultimate Collection* inside it for the past year and searched through a laundry bag for clothes. She got a promotion last year, the first one since they appointed her supervisor in 1990. Her superior congratulated her, then made a comment to her about "looking the part." Years of kissing his arrogant ass and now he was telling her how to dress. Part of her wanted to tell him to pound the extra couple grand a year up his ass. She thought it ironic how she was considered a slob, but the females with their thong underwear and cleavage hanging out went unnoticed. If not for that, she would have just switched cardigans and wore the same outfit from yesterday.

She knew she was a slob and accepted it. This was confirmed to her by her husband, kids, and the landlord after Ruth complained.

Track number four, "For All We Know," started skipping and that was her signal that it was time to head out the door. After throwing some water on her face and brushing last night's gin from her mouth, she turned off the stereo and went in the kitchen to make coffee. She could hear Ruth's big mouth through the connecting wall next door when she turned on the coffee pot.

"Damn it!" she said, slamming the cabinet and throwing the empty coffee tin. Not only was she going to have to stop and get cigarettes but she was also going to have to stop for coffee on her way to work. She loathed the loud music that blared out the overhead speakers there first thing in the morning. Fear of the drive-thru screwing up her order forced her to go inside. The staff there hated her and called her "the cheap lady" due to her refusal to tip and specific requests.

She scoffed and sighed at the person ahead of her that was using six separate gift cards to pay for his breakfast.

"Large decaf with five Splendas and an egg bagel," Janet presented her order as a response to the "Good morning" given to her by the cashier. She made her way to the side of the line and picked up her bagel and exited. Seconds later she stormed back inside, brushed past an elderly gentleman and yelled in the cashier's face, "I want to speak to the manager!" The seven people in line with the older gentleman watched in disgust as Janet berated the young woman working drive-thru and the counter.

"I asked for an egg bagel, not an egg sandwich!" she roared, slamming the sandwich on the counter before demanding her money back. Before leaving she told the manager, "I'll be damned before coming here again." Pulling up to her job, she clenched the coffee cup so tight the lid popped off and spilled all over her cardigan. She went into the cafeteria to wipe down her blouse and noticed some employees lingering, heating up breakfast, and conversing when they should have been at their desks.

Once Janet powered on her computer, she emailed their supervisors and told them about the loafing going on in the cafeteria. Her recycling bin wasn't emptied by the cleaning crew, so she proceeded to email the building manager to express the inability of the cleaning crew to do what they are supposed to. During the employees' break she stood in the doorway looking to report those who did not return to their desks in time. Then she went to the new liquor store on lunch hour and bought her gin there. It was sixty-five cents more than Jolene'Z but at least she wouldn't have to double park or cope with Mike and his dopey nephew.

Returning from lunch she noticed one of the new employees wearing pants that looked like jeans. She figured she could walk the halls and catch anyone that was late from lunch in the process, while reporting the dress code violation. Walking toward the vestibule, three girls shuffled in with containers of takeout food. The one in the middle had gotten mouthy with her a month ago and she had been looking to write her up.

"Ladies, it's quarter after one," Janet bellowed out in the hallway while looking at her watch that's gold plating had all but worn off.

"Oh, whatever Janet, we clocked out at twenty after," the mouthy one called out, walking past her as the three of them laughed heading down the hall.

After reporting the dress code violation to the girl's supervisor, she requested disciplinary action for the three girls. Her manager got up from his desk and closed the door to his office. He blamed her for the problems the company was having with production and told her that the staff was not responding to her inept leadership. Before dismissing her, he commented on her appearance, then pointed to the coffee stain covering her sweater. When she got back to her desk, she told another supervisor she was leaving early for the day and held back her tears while walking to her car in the parking lot. After a quick stop at the grocery store for coffee, she pulled up outside her house. Ruth's husband John was outside talking with the FedEx girl. She saw John pointing to her from the corner of her eye walking up to her door.

Juggling her purse and keys while trying to eavesdrop on what John was saying, Janet lost control of the brown paper bag. The bottle slipped out of her hands and shattered on the concrete steps. She jumped back into her car and sped off to get another bottle of gin at Jolene'Z. It was late afternoon and Janet found a parking spot on the street. Once she flung the bar door open, she saw the same two young girls seated at the bar and a third girl sitting between them with her head down at the bar that looked to be crying. She huffed, approaching the register looking for Mike.

"Oh great," she said at the sight of Gary coming to the register to help her.

"Where's Mike at?" she said, repeating her dialogue from yesterday.

"He doesn't come in until four, so you're stuck with me today," Gary explained, smiling.

"Hey Gary come here!" one of the girls at the bar said, waving him toward them. Once again, she was delayed by the underage barflies. Gary stepped away from the register and she began to gripe. "I'm never setting foot in here again. You can expect me to tell your uncle about this!" Janet barked while one of the girls leaned over the bar and whispered into Gary's ear, looking in her direction.

Gary may have been Mike's nephew but he wasn't eighteen. He was actually twenty-three and had spent the last three years of his life incarcerated for multiple counts of assault. Some kids were harassing his girlfriend at a carnival and he beat them senseless. His mother forced his Uncle Mike to let him work at Jolene'Z on the books, a condition of his early release. In the middle of the two girls from the bar yesterday was Gary's new girlfriend.

After nodding in understanding to the whispering girl, Gary returned to the register. He ignored Janet's browbeating and reached under the shelf and took hold of the .45 his uncle kept for protection. The Irish Mist clock that read 3:45 on the wall caught Janet's attention as Gary cocked back the pistol. She decided to wait until Mike came in and give him a piece of her mind.

All her life Janet prided herself on telling people off and having the final say. On a late June afternoon in Jolene'Z tavern, she had the final say of her life. The piece of her mind was not given to Mike but to the walls of his bar in the form of shattered skull fragments and brain tissue.

The twenty-three-year-old parolee squeezed the automatics trigger and delivered a bullet to Janet's mouth just as her neighbor Ruth's vitamins were delivered a day early. Her body flung backward and fell to the ground. The gunshot echoed in Gary's ears as he looked at the dead body of the woman that got his girlfriend fired from the coffee shop that morning.

Envelopes overflowed Janet's mailbox and home shopping boxes piled up on her porch. Ruth considered knocking on her door to check on her, then decided against it. "Do unto others as they do unto you," John told her when she spoke of her concerns for her missing neighbor.

A week passed and Janet's manager noticed she hadn't been to work. Her absence was recognized once he stopped getting emails from her reporting coworkers' infractions. He called her house and hung up after four rings, feeling he had done his part. He drafted a job abandonment letter and had his secretary mail it to her.

It wasn't hard for Janet to disappear, her car towed, her corpse thrown in the dumpster in back of the new liquor store by her job. Once Gary shot her, his girlfriend and her two friends left the bar, and he locked up. He waited for his uncle to arrive at four. They wrapped her body up in large banners that had drink specials advertised on them. Once they discarded the body, Mike told his nephew not to worry and to keep his mouth shut. The quick-tempered boy questioned his uncle's lack of concern, and Mike calmly replied:

"I'm the only one who's going to miss her, believe me."

We knew little about her
Nor what created her as such
All we could concur
Was her face was permanently fucked
The fuckface woman scowled at all
That came across her gaze
Panting in the summer. Icy in the fall.
Eyes fully coated in an ever-hateful glaze
Then one day she disappeared
Vanished without a trace
Since by none she was revered
What ever happened to old fuckface-?

Scribblings on a urinal stall written by one of Janet's coworkers

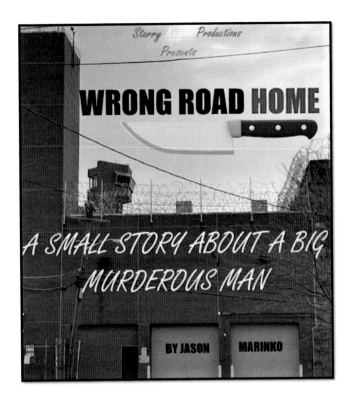

The steel door set off an alarming buzz in Roy Daley's eardrums. He was cuffed in an orange jumper, but he was about to shed the bracelets and hazard gear soon. Nine others stood in a single file line while awaiting release. They were carrying on laughing and talking shit about what they were going to do next. Plans to get laid, get drunk, get high, get paid, and get over were spoken of by all, except Roy. He just stood waiting, stone-faced and stoic as he was when he entered the Preytin Pen eighteen months back.

Roy only had one plan. He wasn't looking for any people to get up with or any home-cooked meal, and he didn't care about getting laid either. His sexual appetite was sated by plenty of unwilling participants during his stay at Preytin. One of them was in the line of men being released. Roy blew him a kiss, providing one final memory to haunt his nights for the rest of his life. The prison clerk gave him his clothes in a clear plastic bag, along with his wallet and a check for the balance of his commissary.

Outside he saw people hugging in the parking lot. He chuckled to himself seeing the kid he fucked on the regular with his lips locked and arms wrapped around one fine looking bitch. Roy wondered if she'd have been so eager to suck face with him if she'd known how many a night he used her man's mouth for a suck hole. The mood outside the workhouse was celebratory and those freed quickly got into the cars of those who waited for them, eager to put the last stint in Preytin in the past.

No one came to get Roy Daley who walked past them to the security checkpoint that led out to the street. Buttoning up the torn flannel he wore on the day of his arrest, Roy gave one last look back at the Preytin Penitentiary and gave it the finger. He pulled his jeans that fell to his thighs up by the pockets and started walking on the shoulder of the highway. After a mile he came across a gas station that had a convenience store behind the pumps.

"I'd stomp that turban off your mother fucking head, if I didn't just get out of jail, cocksucker!" he told the clerk who refused to cash his commissary check. He considered stealing a soda and a bag of jerky upon exiting but was gun-shy. His pace hastened as he thought, "the hell with drink or food." He estimated he could travel a marathon on hatred alone and he was less than six miles away. A teeming downpour ensued, saturating his filthy flannel. Drivers looked at the giant man walking in the rain on the shoulder of the highway with curiosity. Roy lunged forward with his head hunched down like a football player seeking a collision.

"I'm coming Shannon," he said to himself, smiling at the green sign with white letters that announced Middleton Exit. He walked downhill along the narrowing shoulder until a truck had to swerve to keep from hitting him.

"Get the fuck out of the road shithead!" the driver screamed to Roy out his window, his truck idling at the traffic light, shadowed by an overpass above the intersection at the exit's end. Roy rose to his feet and ran in the direction of the truck.

"Come on, I'll bust your fucking hole open nice and wide fucker!" Roy roared back prompting the trucker to exit the cab wielding a small pipe. When he was close enough, he took a swing at Roy who was much larger than he looked in the eighteen wheeler's side view mirror. Roy absorbed the blow with his forearm. Then the trucker lifted the pipe high to strike him a second time, but before he could land another shot, Roy delivered a devastating long kick that caved in the man's kneecap. The fat man buckled under the damage done to his foundation and fell.

Roy snatched the pipe from him and worked him over properly. The same way he laid into Shannon's boyfriend. An act that landed him inside for a year. Roy rained punishing blows down on him. The same way he worked over a punk who tried him in the mess hall. An act that added another six months to his sentence; it didn't matter. Whatever it took—fists, cafeteria chair, or steel pipe. Roy was going to destroy those who wronged him, and it was the last life decision the hairy slob that twitched at his feet ever made.

"This is how you hit a mother fucker with a pipe you see that! Run me off the fuckin road," Roy spoke through the spittle that spewed out of his mouth as he continued pounding away. After six more solid cracks he stopped moving completely and Roy pulled thirty bucks out of his chain wallet, then delivered a skull splitting stomp to his face for good measure and ran.

Drivers pounded on their horns, as far as five cars back, delayed by the idle truck. Roy noticed one of them take out their phone to call the police. He flagged down a cab and sighed in relief as the cab pulled off.

"Where we going?" the driver asked looking in the rearview mirror at the pockmarked face of Roy who was caught off guard by the question.

"Andros's Diner still open?"

"I don't know. They changed the hours a while back. You want to go somewhere or what?"

Mashing out the trucker worked up an appetite in Roy. They would honor any check under fifty dollars at the register, plus he always enjoyed Andros's greasy burgers.

"Eighteen bucks," the driver said pulling up to Andros's Diner.

"Get fucked buddy," Roy said, throwing a ten in the front seat. There was a .38 under the driver's seat he kept for protection and for keeping the peace when his fares wound up beating the shit out of each other and undesirables that tried stiffing him, such as Roy. He leaned forward then relented, happy to have the giant ugly prick that reeked like wet dog out of his car.

"Fucking scurf bag," he said seeing Roy enter Andros's, then drove off.

All the familiar faces at Andros's were gone, his meat was over-cooked, and the bitch at the register refused his check because his license expired. He headed for the door with the green and white check still in hand.

"Sir. Sir you have to pay for your meal." She stepped around the counter.

"Fuck off!" he replied closing the bill into an upright fist.

"I had better meals in jail," he said on his way out the door and headed for the Middleton Liquor Mart.

With the remaining twenty bucks he purchased the biggest bottle of bourbon he could get. Exiting the liquor store, he stole a coat draped over a hand truck. Roy tossed the saturated flannel, then struggled putting on the puffy ski coat. It was two sizes too small. The coat's seams snapped as he shoved his arms through the restricting sleeves and walked on. Smiling as he arrived where he had wanted to be, he sat on a curb between two parked cars. Stalking the home across the street, he cracked open the bottle and took a long swallow. Once he had his fill, he lowered the bottle and focused on 33 Cozner Lane. Roy pounded the bourbon and bided his time, waiting with bated breath for the inside lights to go out.

A year and a half back, Roy beat Shannon Washington and Tom McCreery in their home, and now he was back to finish the job. Last time he stormed through the front door overcome by emotion since Shannon left him. He attributed his failure to not pummeling her enough to prevent her from calling for help. He'd been too focused on breaking the man who stole his woman. In his mind he erred in directing his assault on her boyfriend once he came to her aid. He didn't want to kill her; his only intention to force her to watch him dismantle the man she thought better than him.

That was then. No part of him wished to see her alive now. He possessed no emotion whatsoever. This time no kicking in the front door half-assed attack. This time under the cover of night, he was going to climb in the first-floor window and eradicate them as they slept.

He got back into his bottle while Georgette Chervase got her four-year-old Nathan to get to bed. Nathan never gave her a problem before but was still adjusting and hated his new room. Nathan often reported monsters in the closet and under the bed. The night-lights and distractions Georgette filled the room with did not help. She closed up the storybook, kissed her angel on the forehead, and tucked him in. She crept out of his bedroom and looked in on him once more. Then took a picture to text Mark to show him that their son was sound asleep while he was away on business.

The move wasn't easy for her either; she loved their apartment and her old neighbors as well. Middleton had a blah feeling to it but was closer to the train station. Georgette agreed with Mark despite her reservations for his sake. The previous owners accepted their lowball offer and they moved in the small home. Mark said they got the place for a steal. Georgette agreed but when Mark was away, she regretted doing so. No friends and no one to call, she thought, pouring herself a cup of tea in the kitchen she hated. Her phone vibrated in her bathrobe pocket and before she could read Mark's reply, her son startled her. Nathan ran into the kitchen. He clutched at her leg in a panic.

"Mommy there's a monster in my window," her son said, gripping her thigh so hard he was hurting her. She set the phone down on the counter next to her tea, hugged Nathan, and said, "Ok Mommy's here. Let's go see."

It was a monster in the window. It was not a mythical dragon or a child-devouring witch from the fairy tales his mother read him. It was an infuriated Roy Daley that peered into the child's room. His head dizzied in anger at the sight of the revolving night lamp. Its shapes danced around the bedroom, lighting up the darkened walls with the shapes of stars.

Many a time he tried locking her down by busting inside of her. When he stumbled upon her birth control pills, he beat her for the first of many times. He wanted a child with Shannon, who once exposed to Roy's violent nature, would do nothing of the sort. She left him as soon as the opportunity presented itself. Roy grabbed a rock twice the size of his hand to break the window as he intended to commit three murders instead of two.

Frozen from the sound of shattered glass, Georgette shielded her petrified child. She turned and ran back toward the kitchen but tripped over Nathan trembling behind her. The giant intruder with the tight ski coat lumbered toward her. He screamed someone's name as he clenched the neck of a nearly empty bottle. Roy Daley took hold of the woman who he thought to be Shannon in the darkened hallway. Nathan ran to the kitchen to get his mother's phone but could not reach the counter. "Nathan! Run, *run!*" Georgette screamed as the hulking invader stood over her and grabbed her off the ground. The sound of Georgette's voice confused Roy Daley, who in all his scheming never considered Shannon relocated. Shannon and her fiancée, Tom, moved as far away from Cozner Lane as they could. They even sold their home for a loss to the Chervase's.

Dropping Georgette in his confusion, Roy turned around still looking for Shannon. He figured she or someone else would come to assist the screaming woman at his feet. When he turned back around and spoke out in his confusion, "Who are you?" the point of the twelve-inch steak knife Nathan handed his mother slammed into his neck. Roy attempted to force Georgette's hands to prevent further penetration to his throat. His movements were constricted by the tight ski coat.

In a maternal rage Georgette found the strength to drive the knife through to the other side of Roy Daley's neck. Both her hands were squeezing the handle with strength unbeknownst to her. She turned and twisted it, piercing away pieces of his windpipe. Roy kicked like a man on fire before collapsing. Georgette grabbed her son as her silk robe rained droplets of blood onto her legs and she ran outside.

In the hallway of the scene of his crime almost two years earlier Roy Daley would bleed to death. His miserable existence brought to an end by a four-year-old child. A little boy smart enough to open a drawer when he couldn't reach the phone to save his mommy from a monster. A monster that, once released from prison, elected to take the wrong road home.

Miles north of Middleton Shannon and Tom McCreery stopped at a store outside of Preytin. Shannon grasped a copy of the Middleton Observer and gasped at the headline. Tom joined her after playing lottery alongside her. Shannon held out the paper to Tom sobbing. Realizing the reason for her reaction, he comforted her.

The McCreerys returned to Middleton the following year to visit Shannon's family. It was the first time they returned in years. On the way home back to Preytin they parked outside their first home on Cozner Lane. The car idled and they saw the rusted For Sale sign. It had a banner stickered across it that read "reduced." Their daughter called out from the back seat, "Why are we stopping?"

"Yes, Tom, why are we stopping?" Shannon added smiling to her husband. Tom put the car back in drive and took hold of his wife's hand. They headed home comforted that the monster, Roy Daley was dead.

Next door there was once a man name Roy Daley
He tortured and beat his girlfriend Shannon daily
I lived in this home all my life
Shannon next door was sweet and nice
In moved the brute Roy that she was seeing
A poor excuse for a human being
Roy beat her within an inch of her life
She never returned after that night
A new couple moved in next door
He broke in from the ground floor
Only to exit with a hole in his neck
Mommy killed the monster! Her little boy said
For on that night a human monster was slain
On a damp, dark night here on Cozner Lane.
Had he had any sense he would have known
That fateful night he took the wrong road home-

Private journal entry from Edith McCarthy
Lifelong resident of 31 Cozner Lane

Attic Of Anxiety

The third floor of the Clark's home was off-limits to everyone except Bradley's mother. Every Thursday she went upstairs, and Bradley heard her crying as he played in the hallway outside his bedroom. The first time he heard her sobbing, he ran up to the third floor. His mother grabbed him in the middle of the steps and yelled at him.

"What did I tell you? You are never to set foot up here!" she said gripping Bradley with both hands so hard he began crying himself. She delivered a flurry of slaps to his backside, making his pale face turn beet red and saturated in tears. After making him lunch, his mother told him. "I'm sorry for hitting you honey."

The extreme mood swing confused the child. When his father got home, Bradley asked him.

"Daddy why does Mommy cry in the room upstairs?"

His father folded his newspaper, sat his son on his lap, and explained.

"Before we had you Brad, your mommy and I were supposed to have a little girl."

"What happened?"

"Well before she was born, we lost her. When Mommy goes to the third floor, that's when she thinks about her."

"That's why she cries upstairs? Because the baby died like Grandpa?"

"A little different than Grandpa, but yes. You asked me about the attic before, but you weren't old enough. You just turned six though, so it's okay for me to tell you."

Bradley's curiosities were only partially remedied by his father. The phone rang while his mother was on the third floor. Rushing down the steps, she walked past him to answer it in the kitchen. It was his grandmother on the phone, and he knew she would be on the phone with her awhile.

He always wanted a brother or sister and asked for one for every birthday and Christmas. The request always elicited laughter from his father and silence from his mother, who then encouraged him.

"Pick something else honey."

Bradley wanted to see what the little girl's room looked like that would have been his sister.

While his mother was occupied on the telephone, he seized the opportunity to sneak a peek into the forbidden room.

The attic steps were steeper than those that lead to the second floor, and he labored to climb them.

"Bradley?" His mother called up, forcing him to run back down from the middle of the steps.

"Yes?" He asked, leaning over the banister seeing his mother on the phone in the kitchen downstairs.

"Pick up your toys in the hall. After I get off the phone with Grandma, I'm making you lunch."

He nodded and picked up his toys in a rush. After throwing them in his room, he made sure his mother was still in conversation. He then marched back up the steps to the third floor. Bradley conjured an image in his head of what the little girl's room looked like.

The wall in the stairwell was a faded pink; he had seen that much before. Bradley pictured a room with a unicorn lampshade and stuffed animals. He hoped to see games and toys like a slinky, Lite Bright, or Barrel of Monkeys. Reaching the top steps, the excited boy turned around and saw none of those things.

The eyes of over five hundred dead little girls looked back at him. Black, lifeless eyes in all shapes and sizes. Standing in rows, some were bigger than he was. They were all facing him, and the terrified boy slipped and tumbled from the top of the steps.

Unable to break his fall, Bradley tumbled all the way down to the second floor. His mother called him for lunch and that night he dreamed of falling into the clutches of the army of dead little girls that lived in the room above him.

He never went to the third floor again, but had the same nightmares for the rest of his life.

While Bradley asked for a brother or sister for a gift, his mother always wanted a new doll. She displayed them in the room on the third floor, dusted them, cleaned them once a week, spoke to them, and reflected on the little girl she lost— unaware that her collection terrorized her son.

A Most Malicious Malady

*G*azing into the casket, Maya saw that even in death, Mama's cruel scowl remained. Her tight, pursed lips appeared clenched more than ever. Even in death she looked mean. Maya's mama, Rhonda Belmont was always mean, as far back as Maya could remember. Before Maya's daddy Henry Belmont up and left, he'd joke while playing the card game Old Maid with Maya, "I'm already stuck with a nasty old maid to begin with." Once Henry left Rhonda's hostility became worse than ever.

The emerald ring Maya wore made a scrapping sound on the polished wooden casket's exterior as she rose from the kneeler. She felt her Uncle William's hand on her back as he spoke.

"She's in a better place and not suffering anymore Maya." The quiet pale girl nodded in agreement with William's assessment. In her mind though Maya told herself, "he hasn't the slightest idea of what suffering truly is." William was happily married to Maya's Aunt Mabel who was the polar opposite of her mother. Besides school the only joyful interaction Maya had in life was when her personable and lively Aunt Bel visited.

In the final months Maya nursed Rhonda through fits of shaking from severe dehydration. She cleaned up more vomit and diarrhea than the average person hears of. It was somewhat cathartic to see Mama suffer. It was almost befitting that the woman who was so hostile to her experienced such overwhelming agony. She felt an odd mixture of pleasure and guilt. So much so that she had to hide her emotions at the viewing. Maya was not sad, not one bit. She was elated.

The only other people that came to her mama's wake were the people whose houses she used to clean. Had they known what Mama said about them, they'd be just as absent as her father.

"Just because they have money don't mean they don't live like slobs. I see it every day. Dog piss all over the Richardson's steps I have to scrub. Just because they can't be bothered to take the animal out. Too self-occupied and self-important," Mama repeated often while admonishing guilt whenever Maya asked to go on a school trip or dared to ask for money.

"You think I scrub out other people's shit-houses just so you can go to the zoo? Bad enough I've got to pony up the tuition for that fancy school that's teaching you nothing but how to be ungrateful. I should let you go to the public school, where they'll beat the shit out of your simple self!"

On one occasion Maya committed the mortal sin of backtalk, telling her mother, "I don't need to go to the public school to get beaten, because you beat me plenty here at home." The backtalk caused Rhonda to hurl a hot iron at Maya leaving a pointed scar from the burn on her right forearm. A purple raised bubble of seared flesh showed prominently on Maya's pale flesh. Once she was old enough, she got a tattoo of combined alchemy symbols to cover the burn mark. The ink on her arm became grounds for another beating.

"Maya, we're so sorry for Rhonda's passing. We were fortunate to have someone so reliable and dedicated to work for us." Alma Richardson said with sincerity, her words chosen carefully and beforehand. According to Mama, Mrs. Richardson was "a pill head, drunk, and a slut that screwed the gardener when her husband was away on business. But not a liar." This was evident in her businesslike description of her relationship with Rhonda.

Finding a kind word for Mama was hard, even in death. Once the Richardsons left, the others she worked for embraced Maya with similar sincerities. Always complimenting Mama's work ethic and nothing else, for anything else would be an outright lie. There was one surprise, however. An elderly woman about the same age as Mama approached her with a set of pink rosary beads shaking in her trembling, vein-covered hands.

"Oh, you must be Rhonda's daughter Maya," I women said in excitement.

"You don't remember me, but Rhonda used to bring you into the old Pathmark, where I used to work until it closed down. Oh, honey, every time I saw Rhonda, she'd sing your praises. She'd brag on and on, about how smart her little angel was, going to college to become a chemist."

Stunned, Maya felt a lump form in the back of her throat. She was never the recipient of a single kind word from her mother. She attempted to self-rationalize that the elderly woman was mistaken and had her confused with someone else.

"She probably never told you this, but I was in Malden's Pharmacy when she told Mister Malden he'd be lucky to have her Maya working there for him. Last time I ran into her she told me to go see what a great job you do there working weekends. The old woman continued with her icy cold hands gripping Maya's and as the rosary beads pressed into Maya's fingers, a memory was forced into her mind.

She had to leave school when Mama fell ill. Something to her that was more unforgivable than all the beatings and abuse she endured. Just like her mother to take away something that meant so much to her. Part of her felt she made herself ill on purpose. It was then that she truly came to hate her mother. One hot summer afternoon while she was changing the support bandage on her mother's ailing leg, Rhonda barked at her.

"You make it too damn tight. I can do this myself! I only need you here to call the coroner in case I drop dead. Head over to Malden's Pharmacy. That old tightwad over there said he needed some help in the pharmacy. May as well because you sure as hell aren't studying to be no damn nurse, that's for shit sure."

As the old woman released her, Maya felt a small amount of guilt in her relief of Mama's passing. Almost enough to summon a tear. Almost.

Once it was clear that no one else was coming to the service, she sat alongside Aunt Mabel and Uncle William. The three of them were joined by a young pastor and the funeral director only. The pastor read one of Rhonda's favorite scripture passages that she quoted to Maya often and she felt relieved hoping to never hear it again after that day. She glanced at the prayer card with the same passage printed on it. Then turned to the front and observed the picture of the Blessed Mother standing triumphantly atop the serpent at her feet.

"If it'd please the family to have a moment with Rhonda before we conclude?" the pastor offered. His young face grimaced into a look of regret, for what was most likely the smallest wake attendance in his young life.

"Come on Will, let Maya say bye to Rhonda last," Aunt Mabel instructed. As Uncle William and Aunt Mabel stood over the casket for a final goodbye, Maya dreaded approaching it again. Seeing the tightened lips of her mother, the expression that, even with her eyelids closed shut, still looked judgmental. Smelling the one luxury her mother afforded herself. An overpowering, floral, woodsy, scented perfume that clung to the dress she chose to be buried in was a scent Maya came to fear since childhood.

"We'll see you outside honey. Take your time," Aunt Mabel said as she left the parlor with Uncle William, the funeral director, and the pastor. Maya considered forgoing a second trip up to the casket stalling in the restroom, then making her exit. As she approached the opened double doors, she took a last look back at the sad scene— a single floral arrangement from Aunt Mabel and rows of chairs that remained vacant since she arrived—and felt compelled to give a final goodbye.

She gasped and rushed over and lowered herself onto the kneeler. She leaned in and spoke to the hairless, paralyzed face of her mother.

"Mama, there's not a lot I have to thank you for. I'm sure you know that and if you ever spoke kindly of me, it was news to me. I suppose the only thing I can say is thank you for being so stubborn. Had you had the sense to go to a doctor or hospital this could have gone on for decades I suppose. Anyway, I hope you made it to the promised land you talked so much about in life. Hopefully it will make you a nicer person once you get there." She kissed her mother's forehead and let out a sob but forced back tears, staying solemn to her vow to not shed a single one when the time came, and exited the funeral home.

"Maya, your uncle and I are famished. Please join us at the diner," Mabel offered.

"Thanks Aunt Mabel but I couldn't eat if I forced it now. I just want to go back to pack up the house and get ready for the service tomorrow."

"What service Maya? You told me she was being cremated tomorrow."

"Oh, she is Aunt Bel it's just a remembrance mass. You know Mama, she didn't want any service or anything. I dare say I've gone against her wishes selecting one of the better coffins. She always said, 'I want a pine box and that is it.'"

Mabel gave Maya a look of utmost sincerity before crying and hugging her.

"Oh, you are such a good girl honey. Let us take you home at least if you don't want to eat. Will took off work so we could keep you company."

"I just want to be by myself Aunt Bel. I'm sorry," Maya responded, releasing the partial embrace she returned from her aunt as her Uncle William looked on in disappointment.

"Did you drive here Maya?" William asked, observing no other cars in the parking lot but his own.

"No, I walked. My house is only a few blocks from here, Uncle Will. Besides I could use the fresh air."

"Maya Belmont please let us at least take you home, honey. Since you went to school three years ago, we haven't heard a peep from you even after you came back home. I know you're hurting honey, but I really need to talk to you about something important." Aunt Bel pleaded to her. Maya conceded by shrugging her shoulder and got in the back of her uncle's sedan. As her uncle started the car "Poison" by Alice Cooper played over the speakers until Aunt Mabel turned the volume down completely and turned facing Maya from the bucket seat on the passenger side.

"Maya what I have to talk to you about is important and I'd prefer not doing it in the car," Mabel persisted. In her mind Maya figured she wanted to discuss matters of her mother's estate, what she was doing with the house, and other things people deemed important after one's passing. She was wrong.

In a booth at the Cabrini Diner the woman Maya Belmont knew as Aunt Mabel for her entire life lowered her head while clenching Maya's hand across the table and spoke.

"I understand you will be upset with me after I tell you—Well after I say what I'm about to say." Mabel looked to William who gave her an encouraging nod of support.

"Maya, I'm just going to start by saying I owe a whole lot to Rhonda. And what you said earlier about respectin' her wishes, well one of those wishes was that I keep my trap shut about what I'm going to tell you until she was no longer alive. Okay?" Mabel nodded to herself in reassurance, then looked back into Maya's emerald green eyes that mimicked her own in her youth and prepared to make her revelation.

"Okay eggs over easy with scrapple for you and Greek omelet for the lady and toast for the table. Can I get you another tea, Miss?" the waiter asked. Maya could only shake her head no in refusal as she waited in eager anticipation of what had her Aunt Mabel so distraught.

What could be so important that Mama needed to be dead before Aunt Bel told me? she wondered as the waiter lingered for what felt like an eternity.

"If you need anything else just shout, folks. I'm Davey and I'll be right over."

"Thank you, Davey." Uncle William said in a dismissive yet polite tone.

Mabel looked at William then back at Maya and turned her palms toward the ceiling.

"Hell, I guess there's just about no easy way of going about this."

Maya could feel her heart pounding inside of her chest. She'd been so careful but somehow they must know and worst of all Mama knew when she was still alive.

When was it? She lost her speech six months before dyin'. Maybe she wrote Mabel a letter? Why else would she not want any discussion until she was dead? It'd be like her to take pleasure in dying just to see Maya's face as she went through it. Maya's mind raced so fast she wasn't even hearing the drowned out echo of Aunt Bel's voice, only making out bits and pieces.

"Well, I was ten years younger than Rhonda…I used to get into trouble…She was already married to Henry…took care of you all your life…"

"Enough!" Maya said, slamming her fists onto the table loud enough to garner attention from Davey behind the counter.

"You think I killed Mama, right? Why don't you just come right out and say it Aunt Bel? Only she could be so sick as to sit there dying knowing all along. Damn her to hell!" Maya screamed hysterically, prompting Mabel to get up from the booth and sit alongside her.

"What are you talking about Maya?"

"Mama, I killed Mama," she whimpered.

"Maya, I'm your mama. That's all I've been trying to tell you. What do you mean you killed Rhonda? She was very sick, honey," Mabel said rubbing Maya's back while looking at William in stunned confusion.

The sedan pulled up in front of the Belmont residence.

"You sure you don't want us to stay? You sure you're not upset with me?" Mabel asked repeatedly as Maya exited the car smiling and nodding.

"I'm fine Aunt Be-" Maya said cutting herself off.

"You can call me whatever you wish sweetie. I'm going to come check on you tomorrow, okay?"

Maya nodded as she walked away from the car processing everything Mabel explained. Mabel's words gave a complete understanding of the cruel nature of the woman that raised her as well as a reason. When Maya was born, she was placed in the care of Mabel's sister Rhonda who lived as she put it "a more stable life then how I was livin' then." She was married to Henry Belmont just a few years at the time and the marital pact was made early on that neither Henry nor Rhonda ever wished to have children. Rhonda agreed to raise her sister's child with the understanding that the girl would know her and her alone as her mother until her death.

Maya entered the Belmont residence momentarily and once certain Will's sedan had pulled off, left. She walked fifteen blocks back to the Cabrini Diner where Davey was mopping the floors. She walked past him and sat back in the same booth she, Mabel, and Will had occupied earlier.

"Be more comfortable at the counter?" Davey asked.

"No, here is good," she replied.

"Something to eat, huh? I knew tea alone wasn't enough for you earlier, huh?"

"No, just another tea please."

"Okay, coming right up."

Davey placed the cup and saucer in front of her, and, once he returned to mopping the floors, Maya placed a lethal dose of the thallium salt into the tea. She'd spent the past year putting it in Rhonda's milk, perfume, water, and whiskey, ensuring Rhonda Belmont a most excruciating, painful death in recompense. Overcome by what she'd done to the woman who lost her life and marriage over the decision to raise her, Maya could have taken the poison at home. However just like Rhonda, she needed someone to call the coroner when she died, and she preferred Davey as opposed to the mother she never knew.

IMPACT OF A DAY AT THE BEACH

W aves rollicked and sent a breeze over Todd McCullough's sun warmed face. The sound of jet skis whirring in the distance blended with the squawk of seagulls. Sand filled in the space between his toes as he turned from the ocean to observe his wife, Anne. She was sunbathing beside him, and the sun glistened off the beads of water on her back. In front of him was his son playing in the sand and singing to himself. It was asses to elbows from left to right and he was glad they made it there early.

Todd leaned forward from his beach chair and reached into the cooler at his feet. He took the insulated sleeve Anne had gotten him and concealed a can of beer inside it. The lifeguard to his left was chatting up a girl whose bikini hugged her body in all the right places. "Coast is clear," Todd thought as he cracked open the can and took a satisfying swallow of the ice-cold brew and smiled. The breeze came over him once more and the waves crashed.

He was basked in the beauty that surrounded him as Rosalind Delia threw down the beach chair and umbrella she struggled to carry from her car next to where Kyle was playing. It was supposed to be her weekend to spend with her daughter. She rented a shore house and couldn't get back her deposit so she came alone. She dreaded having to walk back across the burning sand to get the rest of the crap she needed from her car and cursed her daughter for not being there to help her.

After taking a look around, Rosalind decided no one nearby looked like they would steal her umbrella or beach chair so she headed back to the car. Her heavy-set frame lumbered awkwardly in the sand, and she passed some happy-faced asshole whose wife or girlfriend was facedown with her bikini straps off. She contemplated calling her daughter but decided to wait until she got back to the beach. Rosalind felt out of breath as she approached the car she was falling behind on in payments and gasped for air.

Walking back toward the beach, the kid who sold her the beach pass gave her an uncomfortable smile. "Unbelievable what they charge you to go on the beach," she thought. Rosalind returned to her belongings and noticed Happy Face playing in the sand with his brat. Once seated in her beach chair she took hold of her phone and saw no messages or missed calls. She set the phone down and looked over at the lifeguard that was flirting with a girl and scoffed.

Rolling over on her beach towel, Anne fastened her bikini straps and smiled at the sight of Todd playing with Kyle in the sand. She reached for her tanning oil unaware of the teenage boy behind her she had just aroused with a glimpse of her side boob. After applying the tanning oil, she joined her family in the sand.

"Are you building Mommy a sandcastle?" she said, greeting her son with baby talk much to Rosalind's displeasure. Anne then pranced off into the water as Todd went back to the cooler to get Kyle a snack and grab another beer for himself. He struggled to get the straw into Kyles juice box and, when the straw finally went in the hole, the juice spilled over on his hand. He looked for a baby wipe and heard Kyle crying and a woman yelling.

"What's the matter with you? You don't do that!" Rosalind screamed at Kyle who had just accidentally flung a heap of sand over his shoulder right into her lap. Todd hurried to his son who was now crying to see what was wrong. He picked Kyle up to calm him as Rosalind directed her bitterness to him. "If you bring your kid to the shore, the least you can do is watch him," she chastised.

"I'm sorry. I just went to grab him a snack," Todd said over the sound of his wailing child that was getting the attention of everyone within shouting distance.

"He got sand all over my computer!" Rosalind exclaimed, rising from her beach chair displaying her laptop to Todd.

The water was a little cold for Anne's liking and something had just brushed past her leg that felt alive. She rushed out of the ocean as a retreating wave left her in shallow water. Once ashore she recomposed herself, then panicked at the sound of Kyle crying. Anne ran to where Todd was holding her son and a woman was yelling at him with her finger in his face.

"I don't have any cash on me, but I'll reimburse you before we leave," he stammered as Anne came to his rescue and took the baby. Rosalind was irritated but pleased at the notion of being reimbursed. It would make up for the egregious amount of money she'd been overcharged for the beach, and she decided to take advantage.

"This cost me four hundred dollars! Are you going to pay for it?" she howled at Todd whose response was interrupted by his wife. "Your laptop is still working and it's old. It definitely doesn't cost that much," Ann interjected.

The estimate by Anne was incorrect. The laptop was working but it did cost Rosalind four hundred dollars. It went on sale the week after she purchased it. Rosalind caused a scene in the store when the manager refused to adjust the price. Todd was eager to bring an end to the argument and agreed to reimbursing Rosalind. They returned to their place on the beach and got their son's lunch together.

After shaking out the sand-covered towel violently, Rosalind sat back down. She went online and saw that her daughter had posted photos with her friends that she had elected to hang out with instead of her. She looked at the time of the last photo that posted an hour after she called her with no return call back. Rosalind thought to herself, "She has no idea how much of a sacrifice it is for me to pay for her to go to that school and she can't even call me back." She contemplated in frustration.

Rosalind was taking a mental inventory of expenses attributed to her daughter. She rented a shore house for the weekend, bought her new summer clothes with her credit card, and got her a tablet while she was still using a laptop. The tally stopped as she eavesdropped on Anne yelling at Todd behind her.

"You are not paying that hag four hundred dollars," Anne protested to her husband. Anne's voice was a mere echo in Todd's eardrum. He may have been at the shore physically but mentally he was back at work getting shit from the accounts receivables manager. He was thinking about sitting in gridlocked traffic on the way home. He crushed the beer in his hand without realizing it and the sound of Kyle crying brought him back to reality.

"Are you listening to me Todd?!" Anne snapped at him. "You give her two hundred dollars and that is all. Look, she's still using the damn thing." Todd nodded in agreement as nothing he said back would have been correct. He wished they had not come to the shore. The sink in the kitchen was backing up and it would have been a better experience fixing it than dealing with this. Todd grabbed another beer in desperation and sank back into his beach chair. He gazed back out into the ocean and noticed girls chicken fighting atop some boy's shoulders. He took another sip of the beer with the high proof that his friend had left in his fridge and realized in the heat a buzz was sneaking up on him. He realized his wife had ceased tanning and was thumbing through her phone to find the exact cost of the woman's laptop.

The sight of the lifeguard's dangling whistle made him think of the pendulum clock in his boss's office. He started to think to himself about how he would be at work this time tomorrow. He chugged the beer, got up, and told Anne, "I'm going up to the boardwalk to get the cash for that bitch." Todd was desperate to escape. "Start packing up. We're leaving when I get back," he concluded.

"I thought we were going to stay until tonight to eat on the boardwalk and let Kyle see the fireworks," Anne protested.

"The fireworks will just make him cry, Anne. Besides, I wanted to work on the sink," he said, walking off toward the boardwalk.

Pacing the boardwalk Todd looked for a cash machine, his face red with embarrassment. Rosalind was drafting a text message to her daughter about her lack of appreciation. She had recomposed it three times already. She took her Lexapro that she swore was making her fatter and more depressed, then proceeded to call her ex to lay into to him about past due alimony. Rosalind screamed into her ex's voice mail, disturbing everyone in the vicinity. Anne folded up towels, collapsed beach chairs, and covered up the bikini she was so excited to wear with cargo pants and a t-shirt as Todd came across a cash machine.

Inside an airbrush shirt shop, he pulled ten twenty-dollar bills from the machine that would cost him ten additional dollars to use in combination with the fee from his bank. He paused for a second and looked at the old Ferris wheel. It was the only ride left on the boardwalk. Staring at the remnant he reminisced about the time when he and his crush Mary Vallah got stuck on it. A smile came over his face and he caught himself playing out a what if scenario in his head.

Someone bumped into him with an oversized stuffed giraffe and he headed back to the beach. Anne stood waiting on him with a frown, and he made his way over to Rosalind. Unsatisfied Rosalind threw the money in his face in refusal. Nearby beachgoers scrambled for the cash that was now blowing in the wind. Todd snapped and picked up Rosalind's umbrella and launched it like a javelin. He yanked the laptop out of her hands and cracked it in two. Todd hurled the dismantled laptop pieces into the sea like a frisbee as he screamed a litany of profanities at Rosalind who began crying.

The teenager who had been so enamored with Anne's side boob earlier shot the video with his phone. It posted online under the title "Beach Douche Terrorizes Woman." The video aired on local news, was documented in the newspaper, and Todd was fired from his job.

One year later Todd McCullough was in court awaiting the plaintiff Rosalind Delia who sued him for emotional damages. Excited by the decision in her favor, Rosalind jumped in her car and called her daughter. She got no answer, so Rosalind left an excited voice message and didn't notice the red light at the intersection. Rosalind's SUV flipped over twice and she died on impact. The other driver sustained no injuries. The driver of the pickup that collided with Rosalind when she ran the intersection was Mary Vallah. Former high school sweet heart of Todd McCullough. Mary was on her way down the shore to take in the sun, play some games, walk the boardwalk, and take a ride on the old Ferris wheel and reminisce about the time she got stuck on it with her old boyfriend Todd.

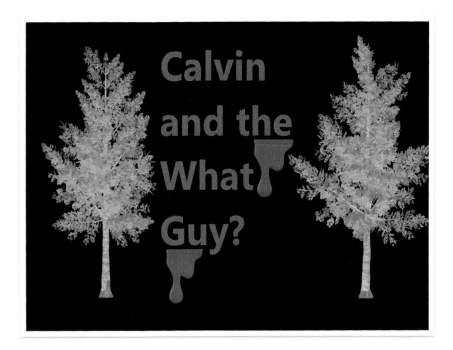

Calvin
and the
What
Guy?

The metal stake thrashed into the loose pieces of garbage scattered throughout Columbus Park. Calvin found it oddly impressive that the single metallic point at the end of the stake's handle was able to pierce not just paper but aluminum beer cans, plastic milk cartons, and other solid items. He wished he had it on him the time Sid Varis pulled a pocket knife out on him years ago. He figured he could have jabbed Sid right back instead of taking off running down a back alley. He and Sid became friends thereafter and it was Sid that took off running when the cops stopped him and a bunch of other guys and cited them for open container and public intoxication. Sid wound up in juvie for setting some kid's car on fire and the judge fined Calvin two hundred dollars and sentenced him to thirty hours of community service.

With over half his time served, he became accustomed to the routine of his mother yelling at him before dropping him off at the park and bringing Mark his service hours sheet to sign and log for him. Not the way he planned on spending the summer, but there was a silver lining in his community service cloud and that was in the in the form of the sun-kissed, tan body of the girl he saw every morning waiting for the bus at the far corner of the park.

Mark was a nice guy and not much of a task master. Once he unlocked the supply shed Mark made himself scarce, then returned for a final survey of the park. Once the supplies were returned, Mark handed Calvin back his paperwork once the hour was up. The park director and teenage boy developed a friendly rapport with one another. They shared a common task, conversation, and humor. Before opening up the padlock on the shed Mark yelled to him, "Good morning, Paratrooper Calvin! Gonna talk to the bus stop girl today?"

"Paratrooper" was the nickname Mark designated for Calvin due to the way he dove out of his mother's car just as it came to a stop. Calvin explained the daily beratement he received on the way over to the park and Mark got a kick out of seeing Calvin escape the car that had barely come to a stop by the supply shed.

The metal garbage can by the baseball field was routinely knocked over, either by a good gust of wind or by degenerates who enjoyed kicking garbage cans over. This was a good a place to start the cleanup as Mark instructed him on the first day. Then it was on to the dugouts of the baseball field that was frequently littered with shells from sunflower seeds and the occasional used condom. After dark those who had little interest in baseball took shelter in the dugouts and the restrooms located in the center of the park.

After cleaning the perimeter of the restroom Calvin made his way to the bus stop corner of the park, and then it was on to the base of the Columbus statue that peered out into the street. Once back in the shed after his first lap around with the metal stake, Calvin would take a second walk around picking up discarded beer bottles and anything else that couldn't be stabbed with the stake that littered the grass. For his final go round was the part of the job he liked the least and always saved for last.

"If it's on the grass, it counts as fertilizer, but if it's on the sidewalk or pavement, we have to pick it up," Mark explained to him the first day before handing him a stained beige plastic dustbin and a half broom whose bristles were encrusted with dried-up droppings. The only thing that smelled worse than dog crap in June was the smell of it in July. The month was almost over, and he only had six days of service left.

Once the hour concluded, Calvin looked at the trash free park with a sense of achievement. He even had a sense of pride in his work. The joggers wouldn't have to worry about stomping in crud and the Little Leaguers who played there at day's end wouldn't be subject to the debris left there by vagrants the night before. Mark took a liking to him as well and told him he was the best worker he had from the courts in some time. There was even the prospect of working for the county parks commission with a recommendation from Mark once his hours were finished. Sure, his friends who either got out of the hours by intervention on their parent's part or were working inside teased him about being the Columbus Park trash collector but as Mark told him,

"What do they know? After all, you're only doing this because you got caught with them in the first place."

A sentiment Calvin agreed with for certain and they wouldn't be laughing much longer if he landed the job with the park that had a great starting wage for someone his age.

The twenty-eighth day of community service went by like a breeze. The metal trash can wasn't knocked over, the dugouts were relatively clean and on his first lap around with the metal stake, Calvin was pleased to see a limited amount of crap on the sidewalk. He had been summoning up the courage to talk to the pretty girl at the corner stop and was disappointed when she was not there. They exchanged hellos and smiles with one another daily and with his time nearing its end, it was uncertain if he'd ever see her again.

There was still a lot to look forward to, Calvin thought as he retrieved the beige scooper and half broom for his final lap. Mark was treating him to a late breakfast or an early lunch at Andros's Diner. While sweeping up some broken glass with the half broom Calvin thought about if he was going to have pork roll egg and cheese or a nice juicy cheeseburger. The internal menu debate in his mind was disturbed by the sound of a hacking cough coming closer from the side of the restrooms.

The gurgling cough grew louder and if Calvin thought not seeing the pretty girl was a disappointment, nothing could prepare him for what followed. For the past twenty-seven mornings he had the park to himself. The joggers and people that walked for exercise stayed on the pavement and moved along the borders, never in the grass. The restrooms were in the grass and the sight of a bowlegged drifter coming toward him sent a cold sweat and shiver up his back in the sweltering July heat.

He noticed the drifter getting off the bus when looking for the pretty girl earlier but didn't give him a second glance. The bowlegged character lumbered closer to him on the pavement, his hacking cough increasing as he advanced. The closer he got, it became clear to Calvin that this guy was trouble. Mark told him early on,

"The cops chase the bums out of the dugouts and restrooms once daylight breaks." This one had obviously entered the park thereafter.

"Eh you! I have something for you here!" the straggler barked out to Calvin while pushing back the dingy black trench coat to reach into his back pocket. There was a large rash on the side of his weather-beaten face and the morning sun beaming off his neck revealed pockets of dirt embedded in the creases of his neck. Under the torn black coat his shirt and pants were ripped and tattered as well.

"Come on, take a lil bah rake fuh yer selve!" he grinned, revealing an inflamed gum line and many missing teeth. He motioned toward Calvin with a fifth of Wild Irish Rose, the cheap red wine swilling back and forth inside the bottle. Shaking his head from side to side, Calvin refused, much to the straggler's dismay.

"Suit y self then. Pretty mutha fucka. Suit ya self pretty light skin heh, heh, heh," he replied before unscrewing the cap and taking a swig while leaning against the wall next to the outdoor water fountain Calvin had been sweeping near.

While lowering the bottle he noticed Calvin walking away from him. His uncouth remark about Calvin being pretty was unsettling, as was his degenerative laugh.

"The fuck you heading to? Huh? I'm talkin' to you here, boy!" he growled, walking toward Calvin, who was sweeping at nothing to create distance.

"What do you want?" Calvin replied in anger, clenching the half broom with both hands defensively.

"I was jest wondering if you wanted to make some money wif me is all. Sorry I ask't." His soft-spoken reply almost made Calvin feel bad for lashing out at him. After all, he offered him a drink in kindness, and it was rude of Calvin to ignore him due to his appearance alone. While his instincts told him to walk away, Calvin did not want to seem judgmental of the downtrodden character, so he placated him.

"Sorry I didn't mean to be rude. Make money doing what?"

His naïve response lit a fire of optimism in the transient's eyes. After reaching into his coat, he took another swig of the Wild Irish holding a finger out to Calvin signaling him to hold on for his response. Running the back of his hand across his mouth to remove the excess wine from his blistered and cracked lips, he smiled. The disturbing grin once again revealed to Calvin the tragedy that was his mouth before he presented his proposition.

"You catch wind of them young boyz sellin' they asses out in Philly? Heh, heh!" he nodded in agreement with himself and quickly continued.

"I was figuring wit my know-how and yer uh fer resh face we could do well fer ourselves! Heh, whaddaya say? Wanna grab the bus back wit me, boy?" he asked rubbing himself with supreme confidence.

Enraged by the disgusting suggestion, Calvin flung the half broom in his direction, which he sidestepped with ease. Surprised by his agility

Calvin hit him in the shoulder with the beige dustbin but did no damage. As the plastic receptacle careened off his shoulder and fell to the pavement, he lunged at Calvin and took grip of him with his left hand.

A warm gust of July summer wind rustled through the park's trees and kicked up his stench that permeated in Calvin's face. As he struggled to free himself from the vice grip of his left hand, the man removed a knife from his pocket and opened the blade with his mouth while shoving Calvin up against the brick wall of the restrooms. Once he felt the point of the blade pressed up against his jugular, Calvin stopped struggling.

"I'll gut you right here like a fucking fish boy! From yer neck down to ya lil baby balls. Thas right, mah fucka. Don't think I won't!" he screamed in anger, pressing the blade into the side of the boy's neck.

"We're gonna go in this stall here fer a moment. Let you gimme summa that throat pussy. See if you got what it takes," he said draping his hand over the boy's mouth while shoving him toward the entrance of the restrooms. Calvin wished the concrete corridor had a door that required a free hand to open. His attacker's intentions were clear and as his nostrils were overcome by a smell fouler than any dog crap he'd ever encountered, he knew if he didn't act he'd most certainly be violated or quite possibly killed.

Swinging his head in the opposite direction of the blade, Calvin kicked into his shinbone and bit into two of the yellowed fingers of the hand covering his mouth. As his attacker backed up to recover, Calvin elbowed himself free and ran to the sidewalk. His attacker gave chase but once he realized the boy would easily outrun him, he took hold of his injured fingers and snickered at Calvin. Then he quickly scampered off on the side of the bathrooms from where he first appeared.

When Mark met up with Calvin at the shed, he told him.

"Sorry Mark I'm not feeling hitting up Andros's for lunch." He wanted to tell Mark what happened but decided against it. Still in shock, Calvin figured that if he disclosed what had happened, Mark may figure he couldn't handle himself well enough to work for the county.

He called his mother from Mark's car phone and was still rattled by the time she came to pick him up.

Shaken from nearly getting raped or murdered in broad daylight, the lecture from his mother went in one ear and right out the window. She carried on about having to drop everything to come get him. Then was griping about her phone bill going up from receiving a call from Mark's car phone. It was all an echo to him; he couldn't wait to get home and wash every trace of the filth that took hold of him off in the shower. In the bathroom mirror he saw a red bubble the size of a ladybug on his neck. The blade had pressed into him enough to break the skin.

Once washed up Calvin joined his family for dinner. As he ate and his parents talked to one another, he chewed his food in silence. That night he lay awake in bed and stared up at the ceiling. He was irritated with himself that he didn't react faster when the knife was brought out. Same as with Sid, he had a better shot of breaking free on the pavement. The blood bubble on his neck affirmed to him that the drifter would have killed him without hesitation had he not broken free. His mind wandered and thought about how he had not seen the pretty girl at the bus stop anymore. Was the drifter responsible for her absence? He quivered at the thought of him taking hold of her as he did to him.

The following morning on the way to the park, Calvin ignored his thoughts of the horror he encountered. He listened to his mother drone on about him turning eighteen and how he needed to pay room and board without rebuttal. While poking at a discarded bag of chips with the metal stake, he was elated to see the pretty girl waiting for the bus.

He approached her and asked where she had been. After engaging in some small talk, she explained that she had gone away with her family on summer vacation.

"I'm Calvin, by the way, and I'm almost done with my time working at this park, but I'd like to go out- —I mean keep in call. Can I call you, um?" he stammered, feeling his leg moving with nervous life of its own.

"Lisa! I'm Lisa, and yes you can call me Calvin," she responded, tearing a shred of notebook paper from her notebook and scribbled her phone number on it as the bus came to a stop.

"I get back from the daycare I work at around four and my parents both work crazy hours so any time after is cool…Calvin," she smiled, handing him the paper that had a heart drawn above the I in Lisa.

"Can I call you Cal?"

"Yeah. Great, sure, I'll Cal. I mean Cal's great, I'll call you after," he said, accepting the number as the bus pulled up rescuing him from his own nerves.

He waved to Lisa in the window and when she mimed a kiss back to the window Calvin walked away feeling ten feet tall. He couldn't wait to call Lisa when he got home, and the attacker from yesterday was a distant memory. After stabbing at a shredded Trentonian newspaper that was evading him in the grass, he looked up and saw the distant memory all too close.

Slumped at the base of the statue, he sprang up at the sight of Calvin and went into his pocket to undoubtedly pull out his knife. The frightened boy took a firm hold of the metal stake and charged at him, like a medieval knight in a joust whose loser would certainly die. Calvin planted the stake into his face, retracted it, and slammed it into the drifter's dirt-lined neck. He pounded the point of the iron rod into him repeatedly until the wretch's movements ceased altogether.

Looking around in shock, Calvin surveyed the area in disbelief. No one was there—no joggers, no motorists, not a soul noticed him. Complete silence except for the flow of traffic behind him and the caws of some black crows up in the treetops. In a panic he resumed stabbing at trash on the way back around the park, all the while keeping a watchful eye on the body bleeding out at the Columbus statue's feet.

Inside the shed he took rags and wiped the blood from the metal stake.

"Calvin, I think there's a fucking dead body at the east entrance of the park?!" Mark yelled, causing Calvin's heart to skip a beat.

In desperation Calvin revealed everything to Mark. He explained how and why he stabbed his attacker to death. Hearing his own explanation, Calvin envisioned having to repeat it to a judge. Only this time he wouldn't; instead of explaining why he had a bottle of Schlitz, he would have to justify killing someone.

Mark's reaction was ridiculously calm. He told Calvin to take a seat on the park bench and relax, then went to his car to use the phone. Minutes went by like hours for Calvin as he waited for Mark to return. He figured he called 9-1-1 to report him and he was done. By the time he walked back over to the bench Calvin was still staring at the body below the statue, amazed no one had yet seen it.

"Calvin I'm so sorry that happened to you. I don't want you blaming yourself! He deserved what you fucking did to him! Understand me? Don't you ever forget that! Look, I'm going to help you out here. Provided you never mention this to anyone again, not even me understand?"

He was confused and scared but nodded to Mark in agreement. The beep from his mother's car brought him out of the state of shock and Mark continued.

"Look your mom's here. Time for you to take off," Mark instructed, then called out to him as he entered his mother's car.

"Hey Calvin! Don't come in tomorrow. As far as I'm concerned, you've performed enough community service!" Mark shouted to him from the shed.

As his mother took the corner and started griping about how he had not wiped the sink dry after using it, Calvin noticed the van that dispatched the city's bike cops pull up in alongside the body. Two men got out, took hold of the dead drifter's arms and legs, and tossed him into the back of the van. A month later Calvin asked Mark while working for the park commission,

"Say Mark, what ever happened to the guy from the park?" Mark returned expressionless eyes and a grimace of a smile before replying.

"What guy Calvin?" Calvin attempted to repeat his question.

"The guy from the—"

"What fucking guy Calvin?! I've got no idea who or what the fuck you're talking about?" The smile vanished and in a stern voice Mark continued,

"Look, I don't know what guy you're talking about, but you better finish up. Aren't you and Lisa going out later? Remember what we said over at Columbus, Calvin," Mark said walking away. Calvin stayed solemn to his agreement with Mark and never spoke of the incident. Until his tenth wedding anniversary while he and Lisa reminisced about the first time they met. Calvin finally intimated to Lisa the whole story and his near fatal encounter with the dead man he only knew as the What Guy.

For in every city and every town,
'Tis a What Guy prowlin' round.
May strength & luck be on your side
Should your path & theirs ever collide
Don't hesitate, there's no time to waste
Remember Calvin and pound the stake-

—Scribbled writing from a piece of notebook
paper found in the Columbus Park

LINKS

L ooking in the mirror and seeing how good she looked, Valerie added the finishing touch to her costume. A fluffy white rabbit tail adorned the backside of her black rayon-satin Playboy Bunny corset. It fit great and if looks could kill, she could wind up on death row. She lost fifteen pounds and none of her figure since she last saw her friends and was eager to catch up.

"Are you ready yet?" Teddy yelled into the bathroom pacing in the hallway. Blow-drying her hair Erika heard his drowned-out voice and yelled back once the blower was turned off,

"What?"

"Party started a half hour ago. We're already late."

"Ok, can you help me with these cufflinks?"

Teddy sighed as Erika always had problems dressing herself. She and their best friend Valerie agreed to go to the Halloween party dressed up like Playboy Bunnies months ago. Erika had put on a good amount of weight while they were in Florida over the summer and was incredibly self-conscious. She went online and ordered a girdle but decided it made her look like a human sausage and was fussing with her costume all night.

"Ok, cufflinks on. Ready?"

"Oh, shit I have to go upstairs and grab the ears!"

"I'll be in the car. Hurry up."

Once Val arrived at the party, she was nervous Erika and Ted were going to cancel. Her phone vibrated in her bra strap, the only place she could store anything in her costume. The text from Erika read, running late be there soon. Val replied okay only partially satisfied. She wasn't sure if Ted was coming with Erika. It would be a disappointing night for her if he was not.

The house hosted a Halloween party every year. What was once an intimate gathering of no more than twenty people had evolved into a madhouse. She saw less and less of Erika and Ted since they moved in together. They only got together for birthdays and Christmas last year and the Halloween party they started coming to in high school.

Ted and Val were best friends all through high school. Five years ago, senior year was the first time Ted introduced her to Erika. Val was apprehensive but she and Erika became the best of friends. She'd never admit to herself that befriending Erika was just to stay involved in Ted's life.

"What is your problem?" Ted yelled at Erika who slammed the car door once she finally made her way outside. She ignored him and pulled down the visor to check her makeup in the mirror. She didn't want to go to the party. She got a look at Val's costume on Instagram while finding her rabbit ears and was beside herself.

"It's a Halloween party Ted, not dinner at the Whitehouse," Erika said.

Ted kept his eyes forward and said nothing. He loved Erika and thought she looked incredible. It was his idea that she wore the rabbit look and now she hated him for it. It was the sixth year they were together. Last year they moved in together. Buying the house was a

Christmas present for the both of them in his mind. Erika expected him to propose and had been giving him the cold shoulder ever since.

The pressure was on for him to put a ring on her finger this holiday season. Ted was looking forward to enjoying the party and seeing his old friend Valerie. Once Erika and Valerie became friends, it felt odd for him to hang out with her the way they used to. From then on it was always the three of them, but he was still pumped up to catch up with her. Erika's mood had him nervous though.

Once they pulled up to the house, she slammed the door shut a second time. Her head down, heels clacking in the middle of the street, with a scowl on her face.

"Erika!" Valerie screamed running off the porch to hug her. Ted observed Erika's scowl disappear and it humored him.

"I miss you guys so much! There's like only six people we know here the way this place is crazy."

"Erika, you look great!"

"Thanks Val, and you! You look incredible!"

"And just what the hell are you supposed to be?" Val teased Ted as he put his mask on.

"I think it's a wolf or a cat or something?"

"Give me a hug you!" Valerie squeezed him tightly. The scent of Val's fragrance cascaded off her bare shoulders. Assisted by a gust of October wind, it invaded Ted's nostrils and permeated inside the rubber mask after she released him.

Ted could tell by the extra octaves in her voice that Val was juiced and feeling good as well as looking good. He understood why Erika was pissed. She looked good in the costume, while Val looked sensational. That moment on the porch would play back constantly in Ted's mind. It was a moment that you never realize when it's happening or even sometime down the road but that was a life-changing moment.

The three of them headed back in the house and things were fine for the first two hours. Erika got blasted and didn't want to go home when Ted asked. She passed out on the couch and he and Val were among the last people at the party. Val admitted to him how she felt about him and they kissed on the porch. Erika saw them on the porch through the bay window and moved out the next day.

Val and Ted never saw Erika again after that, until one morning when they saw her in the newspaper. They had been married for five years and had two kids. Erika never recovered from the betrayal and hurt of that night. Her life went into a never-ending downward spiral. She lost her job and her parents threw her out. She resorted to living in her car until it was impounded after a DUI.

She lived on the street for years and was found dead in an abandoned building. The photograph in the newspaper was her cap and gown picture from senior year. All of Ted's work shirts were at the dry cleaners. The only one left was a French cuff shirt he rarely wore. Valerie decided not to attend the service and was at odds about Ted going but didn't object.

"You need me to help you put on your cufflinks?" she offered, seeing him fumbling with the shirt. His wife's question instantly forced him to recollect the last night he would ever see Erika alive. He threw the cufflinks back on the dresser and left disgusted. In the car he broke down in tears and went to Erika's wake.

Once both kids graduated college, Ted and Val split up. He blamed himself and her for Erika's death and Val blamed him for the death of their marriage. His children grew up to resent him and he drank himself into delirium once he retired. Alone and forever haunted by what transpired that evening when he was twenty-five. In his most private moments, Ted would contemplate what his life would have been like if he proposed to Erika that Christmas prior or if he adhered to her wishes to not attend the Halloween party.

The Mountain That Takes

The manufacturers must not have had Mountain Hill Drive in mind when they crafted this four-cylinder shitbox, Mitch thought to himself pressing on the gas with no result as the tires failed to gain traction. He looked to the left and right of the snow-covered road and none of his options were good. On his left an actual mountain just as the street name advertised and to his right a drop into an icy ravine. If he was lucky, the car would back into one of the trees to shorten the descent.

He tried the gas again. Nothing. The wheel jerked away from him as the car skidded backward. Mitch took hold of it and surrendered, placing his foot on the break. After letting out a nervous chuckle and taking a deep breath, he came to terms with his situation. It was at least seven miles to the closest town. Of course, it would be downhill but that estimate was by car not on foot. He thought about putting on the emergency break but remembered it failed him in a driveway that was not even a fraction of the height he was stuck at now.

It was ridiculous. He had cheated death on so many occasions. There was the time he flipped over that quad when he was eleven years old. Mitch fell off the bike and the four-wheeler went into a pool. The adults would tell him to "walk it off" and the burn from the exhaust would pale in comparison to the Trans Am that flipped him over when he was fourteen. There were a handful of fistfights as well, and he only suffered a broken nose the time he got jumped. The broken face and ribs, collapsed lung, and the pair of broken legs from the head-on collision a decade ago made him a firm believer in what does not kill makes you stronger. But here he was unable to push this car up a snow-covered hill. The only direction to move in was backward.

The tires squealed and Mitch decided he would much rather die than go on from the injuries that awaited him should he survive crashing into the ravine. His mind was locked up with images of being fed through tubes and looked to Emma who was doing her best not to distract him but understood the car would take them no further. She had the strap of her seatbelt gripped with both hands, paralyzed with fear as Mitch stopped pressing on the gas.

"It's not going, Em. I don't know what to do. When I let my foot off the brake, we're going to go backward. The car's not getting any traction."

"Just gun it, Mitch! Take your foot off the brake and floor it," she said, offering the only solution she could think of. Her suggestion would make Mitch shake his head from side to side in refusal. When they reached the middle peak of the monstrous road, he had the accelerator to the floor. Even then Mitch was resorting to inching up in a side to side motion, picking up traction where they could. He considered putting on the parking break so they could get out of the car safely, then remembered the time it didn't work when he parked on a hilltop driveway and had to park elsewhere. This was as bad as it gets when it comes to making a decision.

"Get out here while I have my foot on the brake, Emma," he told her in desperation.

"No just do what I told you. Floor it!" she protested.

"Emma, I've been flooring it, god damnit. Get out here and I'm going to try to turn toward the mountain so the car doesn't go off the side. If it doesn't go, I'm going to jump out as fast as I can," Mitch screamed in desperation. She knew the situation was dire and unstrapped her seatbelt.

As Emma exited the car, she looked at Mitch who felt the car rock backward refusing to be held in place by the brake any longer. He took his foot off the brake in desperation and tried the gas. The rear of the car skidded violently and, even with both hands on the wheel, Mitch had no control of the car, feeling like the captain of a ship that was bound to be wrecked. He let go of the pedal and tried it again, the backward momentum impossible to overcome. Hearing Emma scream outside the car, he knew there was no chance of going forward. The only alternative was to try and regain control of the wheel as the car rocketed backward.

It was going too fast to control and Mitch had lost his bearings. In a last-ditch effort, he slammed on the brakes and jerked the wheel as hard as he could, uncertain if he was steering himself toward the jagged rock-covered mountain or off the side of the cliff that had no barrier to prevent him from going over it. The impact from the crash in the rear of the vehicle flung his head forward. Mitch tried to take hold of the wheel after the smash to the rear of the car deployed the airbag. The last thing he heard was glass shattering. Everything moved in slow motion, then Mitch blacked out.

The chiming sound from the car's service alert would repeat as Mitch let out a groan. When he raised his head, he tasted the nosebleed in the back of his throat and felt his flesh stuck to the deployed airbags bonded to them by dried up blood. He pulled free in a panic and at that moment, a pain seared through his back that took away the numbness the bitter cold had afforded him.

The gifts Emma had so meticulously wrapped and packed for her family were flung forward and sitting beside him. A shattered snow globe that was swaddled in tissue paper was exposed on the floor of the passenger side. The better of his two bad legs hurt like hell, but it was a relief once he was able to bend his knee and feel movement in his toes. Ignoring the pain in his back, he freed himself from the seat belt and reached for the rearview mirror to inspect the damage to his face and head.

The mirror dismounted from the windshield when he reached for it, so he took hold of it and studied his injuries. He had a goatee of dried up blood running from his nose to his chin. When he cocked his head to see if blood was coming from his ear or just smeared from the airbag, he saw what had prevented the car from toppling over. Mitch turned around slowly and saw the fallen telephone pole that was propped up by the jagged rocks through the shattered back windshield. It had cornered the car perfectly and kept him from crashing further down the road.

"Emma!" he called out, able to hear his nasal passages wheezing in his own clogged ears. Still groggy and sore from the impact, he opened the car door as much as he could until it banged against the mountainside it was propped up against. With one foot planted on the ground Mitch struggled to free himself from the cockpit, but he was still pinned in. He hated the puffy bubble jacket but it helped him slide through the narrow opening. Once he was able to rise to his feet, the shifting of his weight broke the car free from its position and Mitch felt it give way, sliding along the fallen telephone pole like a seesaw that had become unbalanced.

The open door threw him to the ground. As he ducked free and rolled away, he heard the heap throw itself into the partial guardrail where it ricocheted, then fell back over the mountainside in time for Mitch to see it drop over the cliff once he got to his feet. The echoed sound of the car's plummet sounded like a reverberating explosion went off in the mountains and snapped him out of his state of shock immediately. He sucked in a mouthful of icy cold air that really brought out the flavor of his bloodied throat box and started back up Mountain Hill Road to meet up with Emma.

The snowfall had become less aggressive and it was easier to see in front of him. The moonlit sky was gleaming off the snow-covered road, lighting the path ahead of him. Water seeped through the mesh of his sneakers, and he cursed himself for not wearing his snow boots like Emma's mother had suggested. Mitch took a moment to catch his breath and looked back toward the fallen telephone pole that was almost out of sight.

It was a miracle! Hell, he had always wanted Emma to get rid of the car and it sure as shit was gone for sure now. Mitch humored himself using his positive thoughts to press on and distract himself from the nagging inner voice in his head that kept telling him he should have seen Emma by now. As the sound of the ground crunching under his worn-out New Balances continued to be the only sound he could hear, he started to panic. Then the dampness crept up to the shins of his jeans and caused the denim to slap into his legs, making him more uncomfortable by the second.

As his skull began to pain him from the numbing cold, he stopped again to remove his hands from his pockets and place them over his ears that were burning. As Mitch cupped his ears that felt like petrified slate in his hands, he saw what he thought may have been a fox or a squirrel's body snaking along in the powdered hill up ahead. Whatever it was, it was the first thing he saw in some time. He foolishly felt for his cell phone that was plugged into the car charger and resorted to looking at his Fitbit that was still banded to his wrist.

Two digital dashes were all he could make out as the device gave him no information. He was approaching the peak of the hill where the car gave out when he saw what he would have hoped was a small animal once he discovered it. Mitch pulled Emma's snow-covered scarf that he got her for Christmas close and stopped it from tumbling around in the wind.

The end of it was ripped and the white turtle design was spotted with blood. Emma's blood. He ran to the drop on the side of the mountain and fell to his knees recollecting what Emma was screaming as her car sped backward. Before he lost control of the wheel, he thought he heard her screaming outside the car, "Stop! Mitch! Stop!" The torn, bloodstained scarf was evidence of her screaming, "I'm stuck! Mitch! I'm stuck!!" The trauma of the crash had made him forget the pull he felt from the passenger side door when he tried the gas again. It was his friend's hundred plus pound body that forced the tension on the wheel.

When she looked back at him before closing the door, the scarf got stuck in the door and pulled her down with him. Mitch held out hope that she may have tumbled free from the car and went back uphill. But why would she do that and not see where he wound up? Where was her body if she was unconscious somewhere? The scenarios played through his head and Mitch would wipe the resting moisture from his eyelids and see faint tracks of footprints below.

Once she closed the car door, Emma felt powerless. When Mitch told her to get out she knew their situation wasn't just bad, it was horrible. When her car rocked backward, she went to step away from it and was pulled by the neck and thrown to the ground. Fortunately, she became unraveled from the scarf that was only in a partial knot around her neck. When she recovered Emma felt the open wound on her forehead and took out her phone to call for help. The low battery signal was not the worst news that lit up on her cell phone's screen. The center of it boldly stated no service. Emma powered the useless device off and cursed to herself following the swerving downhill tracks.

Fearing for the worst she regretted her complaints to Mitch about the silk summer scarf he got her not being long enough. She started to cry and began to blame herself thinking if she hadn't forgotten to fill up the tank before leaving, they would have made better time and missed the worst of the snowstorm. Perhaps they wouldn't have been rerouted by the incident on her GPS. the snow was pelting her in the face and she gasped with optimism at the sight of her car's high beams at the middle peak of the road.

Even if Mitch was hurt, she could charge her phone and hopefully get a signal to call her brother to come get them. Then she became overjoyed at the sight of another set of headlights coming toward her. She stood boldly in front of the blinding beams and waved her arms like a man on a deserted island trying to get the attention of a passing ship. The pace of the headlights rushing toward her slowed down, and Emma's anticipation turned to concern as she recognized the black pickup's driver.

When they stopped to refuel at the rest stop, Mitch went inside to pay for the pump. On the other side of them was a pair of hillbillies. While the one got out to go inside, the other noticed Emma looking at him as he sat in the cab of the truck. Covering his mangy beard with his index and middle finger, he stuck his tongue through the center of his chubby digits and licked toward her direction. The back of the truck had a window decal that read hick life on it with a pair of crisscrossed shotguns below the lettering.

Once she gave the hairy, fat cherub-faced pervert a look indicating her displeasure, she looked at her phone until Mitch returned jumped back in the car. She was about to gripe to him about the gesture made to her but was ecstatic that when he went inside Mitch brought her some Laffy Taffy and a Whatchamacallit, her favorite candy. They pulled back on the roadway and she bit into the treat forgetting about the uncomfortable encounter.

"This guy can pass me but he's practically in your trunk Em," Mitch said in annoyance.

"Oh, the Duck Dynasty cast-offs from the rest stop! Of course, they would wind up behind us," she replied in aggravation.

"Now the jerk ball is passing me. Check out that decal! Think they like guns?"

"Please, they probably grease up the barrels and use them for butt plugs."

"Hey, I'm glad he's in front of me. I'm riding through his tracks."

"You need to turn up here. My phone's rerouting."

"I hope it's not taking us that roundabout way we came in the summer."

The footprints were faint but led to tire tracks Mitch hadn't noticed on his way up the mountain. His pants were saturated, and more blood was spouting from his nose as his body heated up from him running downhill pursuing the tracks. He passed Emma's car and could see a traffic light at the bottom of the hill.

"This road closed little lady. Didn't you see the sign down there?" the driver of the pickup said, approaching Emma with his silent partner cackling beside him while yanking on the straps of his overalls. He knew damn well she was stuck on that road and his candid observation was his way of tormenting her a bit for the dirty look she gave him at the rest stop.

"My friend may be hurt bad. We got stuck at the top of this road. You passed my car on the way up. Did you see him?" Emma said, her voice filled with desperation and fear.

"You see anybody on the way up here, Petey?" the driver asked Petey who shook his head no still playing with the straps of his overalls.

"Uh-uh, Clarence, I ain't seen nothing but that uh Primus back there," Petey answered finally finding his voice.

"Yes, that's my car back there. My friend Mitch was in it," Emma exclaimed, becoming agitated at their casual demeanor.

"Can you please turn around with me so I can see if he's okay?" Her question would cause Clarence to lean back slightly, then look to Petey who would nod in agreement.

"Hop on in."

After dragging himself across the intersection, Mitch's vision was getting blurry. He saw a neon red light on a corner store that he thought was a restaurant or bar where he could call for help. He was trying to recall Emma's mother's house phone number and was disappointed to see the red light was a closed sign outside a travel agency. The tire tracks in the snow filled Mitch with more dread than relief. He knew Emma wouldn't leave him there if she found help, not voluntarily anyway.

"What are you doing? You're driving past my car stop!" Emma screamed, sandwiched between the two men in the front of the pickup trying to see if there was any sign of Mitch as the car passed.

"I wouldn't hold out much hope for him there. That there car had a telephone pole up its ass right next to your Hill-ah-ree bumper sticker heh hek hec," Clarence explained, laughing at his own observation much to Petey's amusement as well.

"I'd like to put mah pole up her ass, Clarence."

"He could be dead! You have to go back! Please, you have to go back."

Clarence took his right hand off the wheel and punched Emma in her mouth.

"Why don't you shut yer fucking mouth and not worry about what the fuck I need to do. Stupid ass New York City couz thinking you can get up Mount Road inna tin can. She's mine first Petey, then you can do what you wish with your own pole" Clarence said while turning up the volume of his stereo. The truck was stuck at a light and Emma was overcome with fear stuck in the cab blasting Player's "Baby Come Back," a captive of Clarence and Petey who had more harm than help on their minds.

Staggering across the street from the intersection, Mitch tried to run to the bar and grill that read Kaye's Place but his legs failed him. In the crowded parking lot, he thought he saw Emma's brother's SUV. In his anticipation he walked past the pickup that Emma was being held in eager to make his way inside.

Inside Kaye's the smell of delicious barbeque blended with the scent of crusted blood inside Mitch's nostrils. His body was stinging from the warmth, and people backed away from the stumbling, distressed stranger. Donald took notice of Mitch from the back of the bar and rose up from his leaning position about to take a bank a shot on the pool table.

"Where the hell have you guys been? What the hell happened to you? Mitch where's Emma?" The trio of questions caused a scene as

Donald yelled, then repeated himself. Mitch took notice of the red and black plaid flannel he saw on Clarence at the fuel pump at the rest stop. Clarence who had ran inside Kaye's to pick up package goods while Petey held Emma at bay in the truck that was still running outside.

"Him! He must have taken her!" Mitch screamed pointing his finger toward Clarence. Donald turned away from Mitch and looked Clarence straight in the eyes and saw the look of guilt.

"Come on!" he shouted to Mitch while running toward the character pointed out by his sister's friend.

"Keep the change." Clarence told the bartender as he crinkled up the brown shopping bag and hustled out the entrance. As Clarence jumped into the truck and pulled away, Donald saw his sister being manhandled by Petey through the back window, struggling to break away from the bear hug he had her in.

"Come on Mitch!" They ran to Donald's car and gave chase. Clarence turned down the radio so he could concentrate and screamed at Petey to stop Emma from squirming. Donald ran the intersection close behind the hick life stickered truck heading up Mountain Hill Drive.

Clarence figured it would be harder for him to be tailed with the condition the road was in. Donald figured since he had the supercharger upgrade to his Explorer there was no way he was losing track of his sister. The driver of the eighteen-wheeler making its way down the monstrous road figured there would be no one else sharing the road and when he saw a truck driving erratically toward him there was nowhere else to go but straight.

The freighter came to a skidding stop as Donald's Explorer slammed into the back of Clarence's truck and when the eighteen-wheeler-s cargo toppled over, it sent all three vehicles off the side of the cliff snapping the guardrail and plummeting them all to their icy graves. The news report read five dead in a four-vehicle disaster. Emma's mother's intuition put a lump in her throat and much to her dismay was correct. She and Clarence and Petey's mother consoled one another after their mutual losses and became lifelong friends forever bound by grief.

Never fully understanding what happened and why their children were dead when asked about the loss they would simply reply, "The Mountain took 'em, and that's all I know."

I n the living room of Aunt Mary's house sat my Uncle Albert on Christmas Day. He pressed on the remote to turn up the volume of the television to drown out the sounds of loud talking from the women in the kitchen to no avail.

"Why the hell do they have to scream so damn loud? They're right in front of each other, for Chrissake!" he announced to anyone who could hear him over the football game and to those cackling in the kitchen.

He then focused on Aunt Diane's boyfriend, Bailey. Last year Bailey joined us for the holidays when he first started dating Aunt Diane. He was an investment banker and gave Aunt Diane the most extravagant gifts for every occasion in the year that had passed.

"That Diane sure has a yap on her! You must have them noise-cancellation headphones over yer place, huh, Bailey?" Albert goaded the fresh-faced Bailey.

"She's louder than all of them. I can't even hear the game. Can you?" Albert continued once ignored.

The other nieces and nephews and I knew little about Bailey apart from the fact that he was infatuated with Aunt Diane and he liked tennis. A lot. He was only a few years older than me, but he enjoyed verbally jousting with Uncle Albert who referred to him as the crooked banker. The truth was Albert was jealous of Bailey and was sick of hearing his wife carry on about how great Bailey was to Aunt Diane, her sister.

"Then this morning he surprised me with a trail of poinsettias that led me to tickets for a trip to Vermont. We're staying at a bed and breakfast! I always told him how much I wanted to visit Vermont," Aunt Diane squealed, overjoyed. She had been through a few rocky relationships after her divorce from Jack, who Uncle Albert actually liked.

"I can't even get Albert to take me to Atlantic City," Aunt Connie chimed in earning a glare from Uncle Albert.

Sensing the awkward scenario that was playing out, Aunt Mary attempted to change the subject.

"Anyone want seconds? I have plenty left in the kitchen."

Then Uncle Albert put on what the family referred to as "the face." We called it that because it was the look he put on every time he was about to say something off color, crude, racist, or just inappropriate.

"That's real good Di. I'm happy for you. I am. I mean I guess the banker here takes better care of you then that Jamoanne or Samoan fella you were shacking up with before him."

"Dave was from Hawaii, Uncle Albert."

"Whatever he was, I suppose he was better than that punk rocker who used to kick her ass. Heh, heh, member him Connie? One with the green hair?"

Bailey heard enough. He got up from the table and hoisted Uncle Albert up from the dinner table. Two fistfuls of the same brown wool sweater Uncle Albert wore every year.

"Diane always reminds me to ignore you every time I come to her family's, but I'm gonna set you straight. Say one more thing to her and I'll make this your last Christmas. Understand me?!" Bailey shouted with conviction as the mashed potatoes fell out of my mouth.

"Get the hell off me you pink shirt pansy," Albert retorted, pulling himself free while my Aunt Connie started crying.

"I'll show you pansy. You care to step outside?"

Uncle Albert tossed his napkin on the table and raised both palms upward in surrender.

"It's okay I'll go outside. I'm sorry. I was out of line," he said stepping away from the table.

"Say your goodbyes, Connie; we're leaving in a few minutes," he announced making his way out toward the kitchen.

Aunt Connie apologized again and Aunt Mary brought desert from the kitchen to the dining room to alter the mood. Uncle Steve made a joke about Albert being Archie Bunker on steroids and everyone went back to having a good time. The loud talking and laughter resumed as we ate Aunt Mary's delicious homemade apple and cherry pies. We never saw it coming and never in our wildest imaginations could have dreamed what followed.

Uncle Steve raised a glass to give his traditional holiday toast and all eyes were on him.

"And we wish all of us best wishes in the year to come. Al, what are you doing?" he said pulling the glass back from his lips.

At that Christmas dinner a decade ago, Uncle Albert pulled an axe from Uncle Steve's woodpile in the backyard, walked through my Aunt Mary's kitchen with it raised high, and slammed it into Bailey's head. Fragments from his skull intermingled with Aunt Mary's pies and scattered all over her white linen tablecloth. While many years ago it's made a lasting impression on every holiday since.

I'll never shake the image from my mind of how tightly he held the axe after bursting Bailey's head open like a piñata. The last words I ever heard him speak echo in my mind every time I hear the song "Run, Run, Rudolph," which was spinning on Aunt Mary's record player when the brutal slaying occurred.

"It's your last Christmas now, it's your last Christmas now!" He stood there motionless until the police came, pulled the axe out of his hands as he stood idle, handcuffed him, and took him to jail. He looked at me from the back of the squad car with a face of sheer amazement mouthing the words.

"Last Christmas. Last Christmas."

I have friends who tell me about how crazy things get at their families' during the holidays and I just nod and smile. Fully aware that no political argument, family feud, or dispute holds a candle to what happened ten years ago on Uncle Albert's last Christmas, the same year noise cancellation headphones happened to be a hot gift item.

*f*ollowing a big screen classic presentation of *The Shining*, Rodger, Marvin, Corrine, and Rhonda rushed into Nero's Pizzeria. The place stayed open until three. If you knew Sal, the owner, he had no problem serving you a beer after 2:00 a.m., while he served up the best pizza in North America. He smiled seeing the four kids rushing in before the place locked up.

"What's up Marvin?" Sal asked while stretching out the dough behind the counter. Corrine and Rhonda made their way to the restroom through the crowd.

"We just came from the Regent," Rodger answered for Marvin.

"Went to see *The Shining* over there, right?" Sal replied tossing the dough.

"Yeah man, we forgot how long it was. Can we get still get some takeout to go? Maybe some beers?" Marvin asked.

"Say, Rodger it's amazing to me I never see you and your friends over here before midnight. You know we serve lunch here too, right?" Sal joked.

Rodger and Marvin were aware of this as they'd been coming to Nero's since they were old enough to ride bikes. Rodger took deliveries when Sal was swamped, and Marvin hung around whenever Roger was working. Sal was just engaging in some friendly ball breaking as he knew they were hard up to grab a drink with their girlfriends with all the other night spots around closed.

"Go grab a table; hang out a little. It's been a hell of a night and I'm almost done. I'll have a beer with you guys. Catch up some."

"There ain't nowhere to sit Sal. It's standing room only in there," Marvin said scanning the dining room slash bar.

"Come on Sal. Just let us grab a case or something to go. We can stop in another time when it's not so jammed in here. Besides Rhonda just turned twenty-one so everybody is legal," Rodger protested.

"Look, the bar's slammed in there but Carmen just brought the check over to a couple in the booth that's about to leave. Get over there and grab it before somebody else does," Sal urged.

Rodger hustled over to the table as the couple exited while Marvin stopped the girls from returning to the counter area from the restroom. The foursome settled into the booth and chugged bottle after bottle looking to get a good buzz in before Sal shut down Nero's for the night.

"Anything for last call Rog?" Carmen, the server, asked happy for her shift to end soon.

"One more round if it's not too much trouble, Carm," Rodger replied.

"Only cuz your Nero's alumni, Rog. I'll be right back."

Corrine tilted back her longneck, finishing off the suds to cool her off, as she always disliked how friendly Carmen was with Marvin and Rodger and felt her face getting warm. When she moved her head back toward the table she saw something. When she set the bottle down, she leaned toward Marvin in concern. She attempted to speak before she swallowed the rest of the beer, then covered her mouth.

"What Corrine?" Marvin asked, observing her body language.

"Don't look right now, but there's this crazy looking guy standing by himself behind you. He's been staring at us. He's been over there for a while!"

"I saw that. He's got like solid green army fatigues on, right?" Rhonda added, a bit giggly from her buzz, as Rodger swung around and looked behind the booth. Sal was turning away people at the door, shaking his head no as he pulled the string to Nero's neon light in the window.

"Damn cuz is looking super intense. You know him or something, Rog?" Martin said after looking and turning back.

"Oh my fuggin gawd, he just blew a kiss at me. I'm going to freak the fuck out! I'm going to ask him what his fuckin' problem is," Corrine said squirming in the booth.

"No! Here, Corrine, take the keys and go bring the car around with Rhonda."

The girls slid out of the booth and put their coats on in a rush.

"Fuckin A. He's coming over here," Rhonda said in a hushed voice to Rodger as she fumbled around in here purse for her stun gun, should she need it.

"Just go," Rodger urged Rhonda as she and Corrine paced away toward the door.

"Yo, what the hell? Who asked you to sit down?" Marvin asked as their stalker leaped right into the booth next to him.

"Rog Carlisle and Marv Dupree?" he asked presenting his hand across the table to Rog. Both of them were taken off guard by the fact that he knew them by their full names and by the rash of irritated skin on the hand Rodger was already committed to shaking.

"Jamie fuckin Tindall?!" Marvin exclaimed.

"Who?" Rodger replied stupefied.

"Yeah man, we played soccer together freshman year," Jamie replied, grinning, breaking up the intense ice grill stare he carried up until that point.

"Oh yeah. man. Jamie right."

"That's right. Middleton Rams in this fucking bitch!" Jamie replied, taking hold of Rhonda's half empty beer and slugging it.

As Rodger was putting the pieces together, Marvin was having a mental recall of a disturbing incident from high school. Jamie was playing defense across the opposite end of the field from Marvin. Marvin was facing the track and football field while Jamie was closest to the sidelines. A parent from the opponents' school was feeling pretty good and was heckling Jamie the whole game. It was the first away game they played. The team was nervous as the Preytin Cougars had a reputation for rough play and crazy fans even at the freshman level.

"Rams suck! Hey, look at this dummy! Ey, look at number nine—he can't play no defense. He keeps digging in his ass!" he shouted to Jamie, repeating the same critique.

The Rams were shut out 4–0; two of the goals were scored while the other team's players blew right past Jamie, leaving him on the ground. Instead of joining the team at the game's conclusion, Marvin noticed Jamie rushing in the opposite direction.

"The fuck you want pussy?" the heckler asked as Jamie stood before him.

Jamie said nothing. He grabbed the guy's arm, swung him into the ground, and kicked him in the head so many times that the cops said his cleats had pieces of torn up flesh in them. He put the guy in a coma. The parent from Preytin made a full recovery so the charges against him were nullified, but Jamie was expelled from school and his family went bankrupt from the lawsuit. Shortly after, his father suffered a fatal heart attack and things went from bad to really bad.

Three years after his expulsion, Jamie Tindall was mentioned again in Middleton High during Rodger and Marvin's senior year. Jamie was eighteen by that time and the story in the Middleton Observer explained his psychotic regression. One afternoon after his mother returned from the pharmacy with his medication, Jamie put on one of his deceased father's suits and covered his face with his little sister's Jem and The Holograms Halloween mask, then hid behind the front door. When his mother reentered the house, he tackled her to the ground, beat her, and attempted to rape her. He was only thwarted by a neighbor that saw the incident playing from the open doorway. By the time Rodger and Marvin graduated, the gossip was that "Crazy Jamie" was locked up in an insane asylum. Until tonight. Marvin was cursing Sal in his mind for not letting them get takeout as Jamie's hard breathing was felt along his neckline.

"So what have you guys been up to?" Jamie said, then cut off his own question only to ask another.

"Was that Corrine sitting here with Rhonda? Damn that bitch is still hot. I used to have to go to the bathroom in school and jerk it strong to her big ass titties. Rhonda's nice looking too. She used to have a fuckin hairy ass snatch under that fuckin lacrosse skirt though. I'd still fuck the shit out of her too though." Jamie let out a nervous cackle stopping himself only to continue in the awkward silence.

"I bet you Rhonda'd let you pound her shithole in. She always used to look at me like she wanted it. Yeah." He nodded in agreement with himself.

Rodger was speechless as he'd just recalled the mother rape thing. He was incapable of any small talk. His and Marvin's silence made Jamie nervous and he felt they were pissed at him and he stammered.

"I'm sorry man. That was stupid of me. Are they like your girlfriends or something? I'm fuckin stupid man. I just get horny and say crazy shit man. FUCK!" he said, then slapped himself on the side of his head eliciting a response from Rodger finally.

"It's okay Jamie. Um, how about you? How have you been?" Rodger recovered.

Marvin was bumping Rodger's foot under the table, making sure he was alert in case Jamie snapped.

"I'm good man. Just working and shit, you know? Where you guys work at?

"I just quit working here at Nero's and I'm going to take some night classes and Marvin works at —"

"Eighty-nine Lumber," Marvin interjected, cutting Rodger off dreading the thought of seeing Crazy Jamie at his actual job.

Carmen returned to the booth.

"Okay Marv and Rog, Sal's closing and he's too tired to hang tonight so you don't have to go home, but you can't stay here," she said with a most sincere smile.

"Unless you're coming home with me, Rog," she teased, clearing off the table as Jamie leapt to his feet and lunged toward Carmen. When she backed away from him, he leaned forward so he was eye to eye with her, his face another shade of red and he screamed, "GET THE FUCK OUT OF HERE BITCH. I'M TALKING TO THESE GUYS!"

"Yo Jamie, chill the fuck out!" Marvin said, exiting the booth and taking hold of Jamie's arm as Carmen fled to the kitchen, petrified.

He yanked his arm from Marvin's grip, let out a chuckle, and looked at Rodger.

"Guess where I work?" Jamie asked the pair, brimming with confidence.

"I don't know man. We need to get going," Rodger said, making his way toward the exit as Marvin was already ahead of him.

"I work at Howell Farms Hauntings right outside Middleton," he said, pacing behind them until a crowd stalled them. Jamie gripped Rodger's arm and continued.

"They promoted me to the final room because I scare the shit out of mother fuckers so bad. Yeah, tonight I jumped out on these three bitches and scared them so bad, they pissed their fucking pants. I'm a fuckin beast over there. I can hook you up with a job over there Rog."

Marvin had heard enough. He wanted Jamie to leave, but the exit to Nero's was bottlenecked. Running into Crazy Jamie had killed his buzz and he couldn't see the girls with Rodger's car out the window, plus it was teeming rain outside.

"Fuck off Jamie," Marvin grunted in response to Jamie's ridiculous idea that either one of them would ever want to work with him.

"I'm serious man. I've got a lot of pull over there, Marv. The owner loves me. I can hook you guys up. I'm in the final room!"

"Yeah that's really good you fucking psycho, what do you do the other eleven months out of the year, jerkoff?"

"I um, I fuck your mom Marv. Yeah, I fuck her," Jamie replied, somewhat perplexed. His eyes widened and he balled up his fists. Rodger cocked his arm back to punch him until Jamie pulled out an old stiletto knife.

"I do, I fuck her hard, and she likes it," Jamie said swiping at Marvin with the rusted blade.

"I thought you only tried to fuck your own mother, Crazy Jamie?" Marvin retorted unable to resist. Knife or no knife, it had to be said.

At that moment Jamie was stunned by Marvin's reply, Sal burst out of the kitchen with a baseball bat and tomahawk chopped the knife out of Jamie's hand. "Scream at my workers, I'll bust yer fuckin head open!" Sal choked up on the bat as Jamie bent to pick up the stiletto. Marvin stole a punch at the side of his head and Rodger laid a kick into his backside. Jamie lunged forward, raising the knife overhead and forcing people out of the way. He raced out into the parking lot and disappeared into the downpour and kept on running until he saw Corrine and Rhonda driving toward Nero's from the Regent movie theater parking lot. He waved them down and Corrine slowed down and rolled down the window.

"Rodger and Marvin are paying the bill. They wanted me to tell you guys to wait," Jamie gasped, drenched from head to toe.

"Wait? Wait for fuckin what? I'm going to get them," Corrine questioned with her last words.

The following morning's headline of the Middleton Observer confirmed Jamie was not lying. Not about his job at least. He worked at the final room in the haunted maze and scared the bodily fluids out of three girls. He conveniently neglected to tell Rodger and Marvin that he'd stabbed them to death as well. Corrine's body was found in between the Regent Theater and Nero's Pizza, stabbed multiple times in the head and neck with all wounds on the left side of her body. Investigators surmised she was stabbed repeatedly and immediately tossed out of the car. Puncture wounds to her neck prevented her from calling out for help and she bled out. Rodger's car and Rhonda were not seen again since that night. Until today.

Disappointed patrons walked away from Nero's Pizzeria as the signage on the door read Closed for Private Party. Rodger and Marvin were meeting up with Sal to go over recent developments seven years after Corrine's murder and Rhonda's disappearance. A car matching the description of Rodger's car was recovered in a wooded area along with a person of interest in the case. Sal's contact inside the department made the arrangements and for the first time in seven years Rodger, Marvin, Sal, and Crazy Jamie Tindall were reunited in the back room of Nero's Pizzeria. A brief interrogation took place regarding the whereabouts of Rhonda. Sal blasted the dining music to drown out the screams, and Rodger held Jamie's head still while Marvin raked the industrial cheese grader across Jamie's face to get things started in what wound up being the final room of Crazy Jamie's life.

Offenders
END

I t was on her to give the signal to take him down. She took a deep
breath after silencing the radio and lifted her binoculars for another
look. The suspect in her sights had already committed fifteen murders
that the bureau could confirm. He was smart and thorough in covering
his tracks from state to state and ready to strike again. Before Richard
Dwyer spilled his first drop of blood he volunteered his time at the
local senior center, donated blood religiously, and drove across town to
mentor at risk youth.

His time was now spent torturing his victims, and the only thing he
did consistently was kill them with a brutal nature that could make the
most hardened killer squeamish. Jennifer Bermin lowered her binoculars
and recalled how she lost her breakfast at the second crime scene. The

sight of victim number two was a vacant warehouse that closed when it stopped making Beanie Babies or some shit. Timothy Jessup had been found hogtied with a forty-inch steel rebar wire keeping him upright.

The sight of Richard Dwyer and the man they were hunting didn't add up, Jennifer thought. They only had his employee ID from a price club he worked at for fifteen years and the pull of his DMV picture to go on before. The man and his crimes didn't coincide. They didn't add up to Richard either, at least not until his ten-year-old daughter was molested and murdered by a convicted sex offender living in his ex-wife's neighborhood. At the trial court records stated Harold Knitrep regretted killing Danielle but in his words, he had to because she would tell and that was his rationale for drowning her in a filthy bathtub of the efficiency he occupied.

That was when Richard leaped over into the well of the courtroom and tried to strangle Knitrep during the proceedings. It took three sheriff's officers to pry him off of Harold. His own lawyer took no interest in assisting Harold and resigned from the case prior to sentencing. Richard Dwyer didn't get a second chance at his daughter's murderer and chose to be absent when Harold received consecutive life sentences. He spent that afternoon at the hardware store.

Unable to penetrate the steel walls that held his daughter's murderer, Richard knew there was no way to get to him and make him feel a fraction of the pain his little girl suffered days after her tenth birthday. He also knew that there were many others just like him that deserved a greater punishment than living the rest of their natural life in prison. Richard went to his local library and used a locator to identify sex offenders in his community. His eyes welled up with tears as he looked at the screen, astonished at how many men like Harold Knitrep lived within walking distance of Danielle's school. He cross-referenced the names with court records and the states prisoner registry and made a decision on his first victim.

He used his employee discount to purchase the electric taser from the price club as well as other supplies he needed and began reconnaissance on Dennis Thomas, who was leaving a court appointed Narcotics Anonymous meeting. It was a condition of his early release from the court that had downgraded charges brought against him due to a mishandling of evidence exploited by his defense. Richard watched him and studied his movements for a week. Thomas went to meetings on Tuesday and Thursday evenings and had a job as a laborer during the week. As Dennis Thomas put the key in the lock of the front door, Richard forced the taser against his neck and shocked him until he was in a state of slight paralysis.

Local police found Dennis Thomas dead in the corridor of the apartment building after the woman living upstairs almost tripped over him the following morning. She switched on the light thinking she had tripped over a package in the downstairs hallway she shared with her quiet neighbor downstairs. When she saw what was written on the wall in blood and the state of the man who moved to her building a few weeks ago she ran and called police.

Steel for those who steal innocence was smeared across the halls of Dennis Thomas's apartment. The same words were written on the concrete warehouse floor below Timothy Jessup's impaled corpse. The victims were in separate states, but they died in the same manner. Once the connection to the killer over state lines was made, the FBI became involved. The Chicago field office was having a shortage of manpower due to counterterrorism efforts and analyst Jennifer Berman was sent to the crime scene.

In five years she was never in the field once. Before she threw up at the sight and smell of convicted child molester Timothy Jessup's innards, her days were spent following money around. Looking for improprieties and fraud and building cases against corrupt politicians and narcotics traffickers. It never bothered her that her unit did all the leg work but never got the glory. It was something she was good at and she enjoyed the feeling of making a difference. Jenn developed a strong sense of justice from her mother and liked to think if Anna Berman were alive, she would take pride in the work her daughter excelled in.

Her supervisor was firm and curt with her but appreciative and fair. He carried himself with professionalism and she often thought of him as an agent that was warped there from the Hoover era. Her gender was never an issue or a problem for him and he came to find her the most reliable analyst in her unit. When her coworker told her he wanted to speak to her, she got a lump in her throat like she always did when summoned. The lump stayed and kept her from responding when he explained that he needed her to assist the forensic unit in a murder investigation in the field. Jenn looked at the frames of his fifties style eyeglasses, his precise crew cut, and bleach white starched dressed shirt and waited for the punchline.

Her boss was far from a jokester but he did have a funny once in a blue moon. She let out a slight snort of laughter, then felt nauseous from inhaling the Aqua Velva scent of his office that stayed stuck with the lump lodged in her throat as he stared at her in all seriousness and said,

"I suppose if you're able to find humor in homicide, Agent Berman, you'll do as fine a job assisting in this investigation as you do for us in the banking unit. We are undermanned at the moment and I know I can rely on you to step up. I'll expect a report tomorrow morning."

She stood motionless and wanted to nominate about fifteen other coworkers that were better suited for the task described than she, but the lump in her throat combined with the fact that the man never changed a decision once he made it kept her silent. He picked up the phone on his desk and began to dial and once he noticed she was still present put his palm over the receiver.

"That will be all, Agent Berman. Thank You."

Thirteen months, thirteen more murders and molesters impaled and skewered involved in a manhunt through thirteen states, and here she was about to move to capture the suspect Richard Dwyer. The fruits of her and her unit's labor were about to be realized with his apprehension thus bringing an end to his violent murder spree. There was only one problem. She simply did not want to.

The circumstances surrounding the case hit close to home for her. When Jenn was twelve, she and her best friend Gwen got dropped off at the mall by her mother. After shopping for CDs at Sam Goody, a man approached them and said he was a professional photographer. He told them both they had natural beauty. The kind that made modeling careers possible. He asked them to come to his studio to take some preliminary snapshots and offered them a hundred dollars each.

Even then Jenn's keen instincts served her well as she refused his offer, telling him her mother was expecting them in a few minutes. She spent the rest of her life wishing she could have convinced Gwen to do the same. Her best friend's trusting nature and naïve acceptance of the quirky stranger's offer led to Jenn never seeing her again. Gwen's body was discovered in the back of an abandoned pickup five miles from the mall.

When she came back to the mall and saw only her daughter, Anna Berman ran through the mall searching for Gwen. The man had murdered several other girls using the same tactic to lure them and was long gone by the time Gwen was reported missing. Jenn never forgave herself for what happened to Gwen. Before that day she wanted to become a veterinarian, after it she only wanted a career in justice. With the full support of her mother, she graduated top of her class and joined the academy. Before Anna Berman passed away peacefully in her sleep, she told her daughter that she was never going to be able to enjoy life if she did not forgive herself for Gwen's murder.

She never forgot but time let her forgive herself. She settled into the financial crimes unit and settled for the desk when she initially set out for the field. The afternoon she barfed on her favorite pair of Donna Karan heels all those emotions returned back to her full force. The local cops and a few other agents had a laugh at her expense. She got a little red in the face, regained her composure, and accessed the crime scene. She spent the evening looking at crime scene photos from the Dennis Thomas murder and the Jessup impaling.

She was thorough and precise in all her reporting and her supervisor recommended to his superior she stay on the case even after the agents aiding counterterrorism returned. After the tenth victim, it was Jenn and not the profiler that was able to pinpoint Richard Dwyer as the murderer. The press coined him the I.R.I. killer (Iron Rebar Impaler) and, once his purpose was discovered, the news and public made him an antihero. Slapped across the cover of the tabloid headlines read, "Rebar Impaler Leaves Eleventh Molestation Vic Fubar."

The pressure was on to bring Dwyer to justice and his warpath had run out of real estate. Since it was Jenn that was able to pinpoint Richard as the killer, she was selected to spearhead the operation for his capture. Outside of a halfway house, Richard Dwyer stalked a recently released pedophile Allen Dawes from a pickup truck across the street. His pattern of using the internet to locate his victims was his undoing. A reverse search on the local database revealed Dawes was being looked into recently. Jenn and her team watched Richard for three days as he studied Allan Dawes's routine. Once Dawes stepped off the public bus on the corner, Jenn felt her heart pulsating watching Richard Dwyer double park in the street and approach Dawes, his right hand concealed in his pocket.

"Okay, he's coming at him with the taser. We're going to take him on the ground. You guys on the rooftop stand down unless we say otherwise," Jenn said over her radio as she exited the abandoned storefront across the street from the halfway house. She and the agents backing her up crept in between cars running up to where Richard's pickup was in the center of the street.

Her radio sounded off as one of the snipers reported, "suspect has already stunned the victim and is pulling him to the truck greenlight.?"

"No stand down!" Jenn screamed, her voice blowing her cover and putting her in Richard Dwyer's peripheral vision. He grabbed Dawes by the neck in a panic, the yellow print of Jenn's windbreaker and her service weapon no longer hidden in the cover of night. "FBI. Release him, Richard," Jenn screamed out.

Under the lamppost on a city block corner Jennifer Berman stood face to face with Richard Dwyer. The man the press coined the most righteous serial killer in American history, the man who never had a mean bone in his body until his daughter was drowned by a disgusting excuse of a human being.

"You have a daughter Miss?" Richard shouted out to her as she motioned the agents behind her to stay back while Richard continued pulling Allan Dawes in the direction of his truck.

"You know what someone like this would want to her if given the chance? Do you?" he shouted in desperation, his head jerking violently as he shouted and prevented the sniper's bullet from colliding with his skull. The bullet shattered the glass on the driver side of Richard's truck, the missed head shot prompting Jenn to drop her weapon and pick up her radio.

"Stand down, damn it. He has a taser not a gun," Jenn roared as Richard ran and picked up the gun she dropped in order to take hold of her radio. Richard took hold of her gun while dodging gunfire from the agents on her right and left as well as the gunfire from the rooftops. He screamed out after a bullet ripped into his left shoulder. Wounded but determined, he unloaded the gun into Allan Dawes's limp body. He then pointed the gun to his own head.

"Danielle baby, Daddy will see you soon." He closed his eyes and squeezed the trigger as the gun clicked hollow, its chamber empty. Jenn tackled Richard off the curb and onto the blacktop. Bringing an end to the hail of bullets, she took hold of his taser and stunned him with her knee placed firmly in his back. Jenn put handcuffs on him as Richard repeated,

"Steel for those who steal innocence" the entire way to Merci hospital where he was treated for the gunshot to his shoulder. Richard Dwyer's trial was one of the strangest in American history. Once he refused to plead insanity, the defense resorted to using statements from loved ones thanking him for giving them the justice the courts could not. Against defense strategy protocol he took the stand in his own defense and elicited tears from judge and jury alike as he explained his daughter's tenth birthday party and the loss he suffered following it. Not a single soul spoke for his victims, a point repeated in the closing arguments by his defense counsel. Agent Jennifer Berman wept quietly in the back of the courtroom as well and exited the courtroom before the verdict was read.

She hustled down the side of the courthouse steps to avoid the blitz of reporters huddled in the center of the entrance. After wiping the tears from her cheeks, she saw a young girl holding hands with her friend look back and smile at her. Jenn smiled back and headed home to Chicago.

She walked into her supervisor's office for the first time without being summoned in six years of working there and gave him her resignation, typed up moments before she stepped into the Aqua Velva lair. He removed the nineteen fifties frames and rose to his feet and extended his hand to her. They shook hands and he did not protest her resignation but thanked her and requested she take a few weeks off to reconsider.

Happy to take a shower in her own place for the first time in a long time, Jennifer Berman put on her robe and after making herself a cup of tea sat down at her computer and typed Gwendolyn Jacobs Cold Case into the search engine. She took a sip of her tea and clicked on the link that brought up information on Gwen and several other girls and said aloud to herself,

"Steel for those who steal innocence."

LIFTED

N ever was the urge to kill so present or the feeling so strong. Reggie was sick and tired. Damn tired. Earlier that day when he drove to the doctor on his lunch hour, his car overheated. A coworker dropped him off at home and his mind spiraled on how he was going to make it to his second job. The busses only ran on the main road, and he'd never make it for second shift if he walked where it let him off. Calling out sick wasn't an option.

Scrolling through the menu of his phone, Reggie found the Lifter ride app he used the last time his car failed him. The estimate had him at the warehouse in twenty minutes and pickup in less than five. He sent the payment and rushed to his refrigerator to get some food. The doctor called in a prescription for the pink eye that had his eye shuttered closed. He wanted to hit the pharmacy on the way into the Time Co. Warehouse, get the antibiotic, and start his second shift. The cost of his ride would be double if he elected to stop at the pharmacy first and the way Reggie saw it, he'd be losing money going to work with the additional stop.

His phone sounded once he raised the fork to his mouth. He dropped it in disgust and ran out the door.

"Okay, so we're going to Time Co. Warehouse?" Maria, the girl who came to pick him up, asked. The car she came to get him in was a sport sedan and the interior's scent was a combination of floral fragrance and new car smell.

"Yes, but I work in the shipping yard way down the road from the main building."

"Not a problem. Have you there in a few minutes."

Reggie removed his glasses as the sun came down in the back seat. His infected eye itched without mercy but he resisted scratching it. Maria caught a glimpse of him in the rear view.

"Hey, are you okay? That looks really bad."

"At my daytime job they hire temporary staff that don't get paid if they take off sick, and a girl I work with had pink eye for the past week and passed it on to me."

"Damn that sucks. You probably shouldn't go into your other job here."

"Funny thing is I can't take any time off from my part-time and my shift supervisor is always looking for a reason to mess with me. Damn, this itches so bad."

"Well, here we are. Hope your night goes better."

Reggie gave a nod and a smile as he exited the sedan. He took out his phone and gave Maria a positive rating and a seven-dollar tip he really couldn't afford, but since she was professional, concerned, and courteous, he extended himself.

On the way in Reggie noticed something odd—all the parking spaces were vacant where he normally parked his car.

"Good thing I'm early. Probably shorthanded tonight," he said to himself while putting in his earphones and making his way through the lobby. Reggie planned to listen to some instrumental music tonight to relax his mind while working. Forget about how much it was going to cost to fix the car and how and when he was going to pick up the antibiotic and eye drops at the pharmacy. Just make it through the shift and put this day in the books. Coming across some Beethoven he was about to select, something else odd came to his attention.

There was no sound of forklifts beeping through the aisles, no one in the break room talking, and the girl who worked reception upfront was gone when he came in as well. Approaching his workstation, his shift supervisor stood with a facial expression more unpleasant than usual.

"What's going on Ken? Where is everybody?"

"Oh damn Reg, we were supposed to call everyone before they reported. I couldn't find your number. We're done; company's bust. Whatever you got here, take it home with you because the place will be locked up tomorrow. What's wrong with your eye?"

"What do you mean bust?"

"Just what I said, company's bust and folding. Word came down from up top to tell everyone to pack it in."

"Bullshit."

"Excuse me?"

"You've called me five times since I worked here Ken. Remember when I was in the bathroom and you were ready to write me up for leaving my station? Johnny told me. You've been a dick to me since my first day here and you let everyone else but me know we were closed on purpose. Bullshit."

Ken let out a nervous chuckle, preparing to choose his next words carefully. He was no longer Reggie's supervisor and he didn't have to explain anything more to him. He smirked and walked past him, then stopped a few steps away. He dropped the box of his personal effects and started back toward Reggie.

"You know what? If I've been a dick to you, I can tell you why because it doesn't matter now. I don't like looking at your ghetto ass coming in here with your cornrows, laughing and joking with the other degenerates that work for me, on break smoking your Black and Milds, pitching quarters by the dumpster like the derelicts youse are. So fuck you, because hiring losers like you is probably the reason this company's going under and I'm out of a job."

Reggie nodded in understanding, a bit overcome by Ken's honesty. He wanted to kick Ken's ass but was too mentally fatigued by previous events to summon the energy. Ken stood waiting for a response and when none was given, went to pick the box back up. Reggie snapped and paced toward Ken who expected him too. He turned around and slammed his fist right into Reggie's infected eye. Reggie staggered back and covered his face with his hand. "That's what you get," Ken said, then picked the box back up and walked on.

A dozen thoughts circled in Ken's mind—the mortgage, the braces his kid needed, his stepdaughter in rehab followed by the punk he just hit calling the cops on him. His thought raced with his movements so quickly he never heard the beeping. Cold metal slammed into his kidneys and his shirt pressed into his flesh, a tire flattened his arm into the warehouse floor. Ken's screams echoed throughout the empty warehouse as his body buckled under over five thousand pounds of pressure. Yelling turned to crying as Reggie steered forward and put the lift in reverse. "That's what I get, huh Ken?" Blinding rage in his pulsating eye. On the way back over, Ken's skull burst under the forklift.

Outside the warehouse Reggie trembled, waiting for his ride back. The picture frame that spilled out of the box with pictures of Ken's wife and kids made him feel like he was going to puke. The driver couldn't find the warehouse, so Reggie walked out to the main road. He finally got in the back of the crossover vehicle and was greeted by Hammad. Rather than the floral, new car scent of Maria's ride, Hammad's reeked of body odor and curry. Reggie's mind was in a tailspin as Hammad asked him questions at a rapid pace.

"What work you do here? What's wrong with your eye? Why you no have right address for pickup on app?" Panic set in for Reggie. He knew he crushed Ken with the forklift in one of the blind spots of the warehouse's security cameras but wasn't sure if they picked up sound. Hammad's rapid line of questioning had him playing out a scenario in his head.

One where the police were questioning Hammad who gave them rapid fire answers about Reggie.

"Yes, I pick him up in road by building where the dead man was. He say not much with eye all swollen and his hands shaking." Never was the urge to kill so present or the feeling so strong. Hammad answered his Bluetooth device and spoke rapidly in his native language. The faster he spoke, the faster he drove. The car approached the highway exit turn-off ramp at fifty miles per hour faster than the turn was to be made at. This was not Hammad's doing. Reggie lunged forward from the back seat and, with the wires from his earphones doubled over, choked Hammad with all his might. The driver let go of the wheel with both hands grabbing at his neck. His right foot stepped into the accelerator and the car careened over the highway embankment, flipping over itself once it hit the ground. And this is how Reggie, Ken, and Hammad were all lifted to death on that fateful day that the Time Co. Company went out of business.

Boarder In The Floorboards

I worked with the old chap years ago. He was a jovial, good-spirited soul with youthful exuberance for his advanced age. His position, a salesman and I a manager for the credit given to his clients. We shared work and humor together until I pursued other avenues. How I wish our relationship ended there. If so, I could have remembered him as the refined, good-natured, humorous fellow from those days.

Years passed and our paths crossed at the market or public library. He was now propped up by a cane and his dress was more casual than business. Even in his hobbled state, he still towered over me, a large hulking mass of a man. We'd exchange pleasantries each time we came to see one another. I noticed the old man's regression becoming more evident with each encounter. His once piercing blue eyes were now a fading gray and his skin had become spotted and jaundiced. "I've given up the advertising business and opted for early retirement!" he proclaimed and to that I wished him well.

Following that encounter, a mutual acquaintance of the old man and myself reached out to me and reported on his decline. He lived in a place with too many steps for his hobbled legs to travel and asked if I'd offer lodging to ease his burdens. I quickly accepted and the troubles began When he surveyed the guest dwelling, it was not to his liking.

"This room is too small," he growled in the surliest voice. Sympathetic to his request, I offered a choice.

Not take it or leave it. I'm far too kind for that. I offered the master bedroom, then helped him pack.

'Twas then my decision came into question. In his residence prior sat his possessions.

Encapsulated in dirt and peppered with dust. His metals corrosive, encrusted in rust.

Ragged bedsheets yellowed from years of grime; they'd not seen the wash in a very long time.

What could I do? Renege upon my original offer?

'Twould not be proper, 'twould not be right, and as stated earlier, I'm far too polite.

Into my bedroom sat his filthy possessions. Was he filthy as well? That was the question.

It's important to relay that living with me also was a female guest. Upon meeting the old man, she did not protest.

She dusted his lampshades and cleared out some space for the gray-eyed boarder to move into the place.

We cohabitated in peace for a couple of weeks. We barely saw him, and he'd seldom speak. Hello, goodbye, brief how-do-you-dos.

On the first he paid the coming month's dues. That month he wore the same hat, the same clothes and shoes that were never removed.

The boarder was asleep by the time I got home. I'd hear his dreams haunt him, in his whimpering groans. At times, he'd shout out in the dead chilling fright, after we'd pass one another like ships in the night.

One mid-Saturday the boarder stormed in as I was cleaning the bath, levying a litany of grievances, scolding with wrath.

"I can't use this shower unless it has handles."

"I can't sleep at night when you're watching TV."

"I dislike the aroma of your scented candles."

"This residence is proving most unpleasant to me!" said the gray-eyed, growling curmudgeon.

I fell back on my experience using a drill and installed iron handles to meet with his will.

Installed a rack for his bath towel as well. The towel undampened, his chambers beginning to smell.

I lowered my volume so he could rest, relieved he'd gotten this off of his chest.

At times, the woman and I would play fight, wrestling one another in the living room at night.

Headlocks and leglocks till one would submit. The gray-eyed boarder slept through all of it.

His hearing quite bad, his sleep quite deep. How was he disturbed from sounds made by me?

The summer months were upon us, and the towel still bone dry. "Your friend never washes. Please ask him why," pleaded the woman, as the stench was malodorous, we kept his door closed as the odor became quite onerous. Her complaints increased as did the foulness from the master bedroom. I'd pass my own corridor holding my breath. Appeasing the gray-eyed dirt merchant's every request.

Because, as I told you, I'm far too polite.

My home grew unstable from the dirty old man. We increased ventilation and sped up the fan. The woman's complaints continued but only to me, as she feared the gray-eyed giant that screamed in his sleep. My politeness would remedy the situation no further; we had to dissipate. I was prepared to tell the gray-eyed filth collector he must vacate. He came home that evening uncharacteristically late. His Velcro white shoe was saturated in blood. I grabbed the first aid kit to patch him up. The yellow skin of his leg burst open and spouted blood on my rug. I sat him up and inspected the wound and made a fatal error and leaned in too soon. I removed his shoe and his bloodstained sock and detected an odor I've since not forgot.

The smell from his bloodied foot and leg caused me to gag and discharge my stomach into my own mouth. The wrathful stench was that of a dead skunk infected with gout. Gaining my composure, I bandaged him up, raced to my bathroom, and violently threw up.

In the days following, the gray boarder learned his toes had to be amputated due to an unattended infection. I could not expect him to relocate missing toes and I delayed his ejection.

I blinded myself to his repugnant habits in order to preserve our past friendship. One late afternoon I sat in my study to avoid the wretched scent of the boarder and the never-ending complaints of the woman. I gazed out my study and a red-breasted robin crept up to my windowsill and, to my terrified amazement, it squawked at me.

"I am the spirit of the previous owner of this house. That dirty old boarder, you must throw him out." I leapt backward in shock and gasped as the enchanted creature continued, "if he is still here in the next coming day, all in my house shall discover what true suffering's about!" The robin took flight and left me troubled and trembling. I went out for a walk. Then the woman began harassing me, "he is remiss of hygiene, putting our own health at risk. His toes had to be amputated. I cannot bear this!" I hurried outside, slamming the door shut.

I stormed out of the house and made my way down the street, then the enchanted robin cawed out to me, "I haunt your boarder and poison his dreams. I want him gone from my home. You must make him leave!"

When I returned home hours later, the woman smiled saying,

"The boarder has departed; he's taken his leave."

"What of his furniture? It's still in his room."

"He told me he'd send for them one day soon. He said you were nasty, unaccommodating, and rude. He said you had a bad attitude."

"That gray-eyed dirty bastard," I said in deep dread. "His stench was so foul he disturbed the dead!"

"Disturbed the dead?" questioned the woman of me. I said, "never mind. I'm glad he's taken leave."

I sat in my study, cognac in hand, enjoying a cigar, bidding good riddance to the man. My euphoric moment was brief, much to my chagrin, as the robin intruded upon my window yet once again.

"Away foul beast! Haunt me no more! The dirt merchant boarder no longer darkens my door!"

"His stinking bones still creak upon my foundation. Prepare for my wrath and utmost devastation!"

"Be gone treacherous bird, survived out of sheer damnation!"

I hurled my snifter at the lying bird and he fluttered away. I'd no longer listen to what the foul beast would say.

I grabbed another glass and drank until I was drunk. then rose the scent of that gout-ridden skunk.

Then came the groans he'd let out in his sleep. From under his room's floorboards I heard him speak!

"You ended my life in the twilight of my years." I climbed to my feet to see his position, then the bastard demon bird entered through the window's partition. The red-breasted bird chirped in concert with the moans of the old man. The voices blended and echoed. vibrating my skull over and over again. "I shall see that you suffer, see that you suffer."

"Silence, you demons, silence!"

The woman burst into my study to answer my screams. She placed calming hands upon my back, then slipped in a puddle of spilled-out cognac.

Her body flung forward on the hardwood floor. she fell headfirst and then was moving no more.

"Dead as can be," the bird cackled to me. "I told you I would make you suffer if you did not adhere to my wish. Look what's happened to you because of all this!"

"The old man has left, Robin. What more do you wish? This innocent woman's dead. Explain, I insist!"

"Dead, yes. Innocent, no. The dirty boarder remains under your floor. She murdered him when you ran out of the door. She stabbed him to death while he was asleep, then wrapped him up in those dirty yellow sheets. She then buried him under the floorboards of this house. That's why you heard him when you awoke from your stupor. Now go answer the door for officers McGinn and Cooper."

I attempted to gather myself as my head was reeling. Then a droplet of blood fell from the ceiling. I looked up from the place where the gray-eyed boarder had laid and my ceiling confirmed that he was, in fact, slayed. The woman had covered up every aspect of the deed but neglected the ceiling, which was blood splattered indeed.

"That's what you get!" The bird squawked and went to take leave. Then a feral cat pounced and took the bird's neck in its teeth. They broke down the door and took me away. As I was cuffed they uncovered the yellow sheets. The boarder's gray, dead eyes gazed back at me. **Murderer Kills Woman, Puts Boarder under Floorboards** the newspaper said. "A most despicable indictment!" in the courtroom I uttered in dread. The jury deliberated in record time and sentenced me to death for a most heinous crime. As I march to my death with my very last breath I'll say my last words, "with all due respect, I maintain my innocence as I go to my death on this night as the only crime I've committed was that I'm far too polite."

Basements and bedrooms of homes made long ago
House horrible memories you'd prefer to not know
Someone's definitely been killed where you're living now
If not in your home, then on your property's grounds
Foundations are layered with blood from before
Something to inquire upon prior to settling for sure
Be wary of beasts that speak for the dead
For it may be upon you they levy their dread-

—Written by Lyle Almstead, a.k.a. the kind killer landlord, prior to his execution previously printed in the Middleton Observer

HALLOWEEN HURRICANES

My father passed away in April of 2012, and I looked for distraction wherever I could find it. In late August of that same year, I took on a secondary job as a newspaper courier. I was familiar with the location as I'd done work there some years earlier when extra income was needed. Sometimes I'd arrive at the depot to pick up my papers as early as one in the morning. A herd of sleep-deprived carriers in line waited with me for *New York Times, Post, Wall Street Journal, Trenton Times, Trentonian* and the worst of them all, that was late every day, *Philadelphia Star Ledger.* Frequently the other carriers purchased the ledger while out on their routes to save time. Every morning from August to October that year, seven days a week, I stood shoulder to shoulder with a woman who never smiled and her body language screamed angst and irritation.

She was always there first and if I happened to be in front of her, she cut away to the front of the line. If anyone spoke up to her, she said nothing back. Every morning she wore a permanent frown, wire-rimmed glasses, the same light blue winter poncho, and the boots you'd expect to see on a hipster or yuppie that celebrate the L.L Bean catalogue. An odd selection for a black woman in her fifties for certain. We referred to her as "The Duck Boot Woman."

Months passed and I avoided the Duck Boot Woman, always letting her snatch up her bundles off the counter before me Age before beauty and all that. I made a few friends on the job and we engaged in conversation while bagging up our papers before heading out on our separate routes. The warehouse was full of interesting characters aplenty and when discussion wasn't about sports, movies, or the 2012 presidential election, gossip was frequent between the six of us. We joked and laughed among ourselves and shared stories of crazy customers and complaints.

October came and went and I'd become accustomed to working every day of the week and accepted life with no days off. My primary concern was my piece of garbage car that failed me frequently during the route. The extra income I earned went to gas, which soared to almost five dollars a gallon, and repairing the red piece of crap I got around in. I took on a fall semester of night school classes and never noticed that the Duck Boot Woman was missing from my morning routine. Hurricane Sandy hit New Jersey hard, disrupting all our routes and Halloween. The storm was so bad we were told not to come in to deliver our papers. The morning after the hurricane we were given both days' deliveries. Being independent contractors, this was good as we were able to make up the lost pay. What was bad was navigating through my route in Princeton. Fallen trees blocked off main roads and, when I finally got into town, the only light came from the headlights of my red shitbox and the only sound you could hear was the whirr of generators. Often when I walked up the catwalk and checked in, there were requests for donations, be it kids school candy fundraisers, church causes, and so on. In addition to being a full-time government employee, a part-time news courier, pirated movie and marijuana salesman, and running a weekly lottery, I had no extra money. I'd glance at them briefly, then pick up my list of route changes and complaints and go about my business.

The distraction of the hurricane brought me to an unwelcome stop. No classes to go to, day job closed for state of emergency, not even the seven day a week paper job to go to. I sat in my apartment with no electricity, cursed with a day to do nothing but spend some time in my own head. The stoppage allowed me to focus on the fact that my father was deceased. I tried to sleep, but the seven comforters I piled atop me were no match for the cold that kept me awake and thinking. Thanksgiving was coming and, for the first time in my life, he wasn't going to be alive for it. We were to report back to the warehouse the next day, so it's no wonder I took little notice of the white cardboard sign with a woman's picture that read R.I.P. in the area reserved for fundraisers and causes.

My other six friends were all in a hurry to navigate through the hellish delays that awaited us all, so there was little time for discussion. Hurricane recovery was going on everywhere as we prepared for Thanksgiving holiday inserts and the busiest and bulkiest newspapers of the year. Many of us sent holiday cards to our customers with stamped return envelopes, anticipating yearly gratuities from those that stiffed us most of the year. 2008 recession or not, if you don't have the money to tip the person bringing things to your door, you have no business having anything dropped at your door. Get it yourself. In all the hurricane recovery and holiday anticipation I never noticed The Duck Boot Woman was absent from my everyday routine. After a few days I figured she quit or got fired; the job had a high turnover rate to begin with.

The year ended and, after scrimping together a down payment for a house, I moved myself from my apartment to my new house Christmas week. I was too fatigued to move in until New Year's Eve. I talked with my friends at the paper job about being sick of driving out to Princeton and my displeasure with my route that couldn't be more inconvenient in location from the depot or where I lived. Routes were always a hot topic: picking up more routes, making more money, and so on. Rich, who bagged up across the standing cubicle from me, nodded in understanding and then said in response to my complaint,

"You should try to get Sharon's route. It's down again after somebody took it over."

"Where at? Who was Sharon?" I questioned.

"The Ewing Route! Sharon! You know! The lady that died last year!"

I was puzzled. Rich looked to the ceiling in frustration of my failing recall. I had no idea who the hell he was talking about and where this good route in Ewing was.

"Died? You mean the woman they had the collection for after the hurricane?"

"Yes!"

"I didn't even recognize that woman in the picture. Where did she bag up her papers?"

"She never bagged them up. She took them to her house. But she looked good in her picture, nothing like when we saw her here. Jason you'd be standing in line with her every morning when I came in."

I made a face of understanding who he was talking about and we both said it out loud at the same time.

"The Duck Boot Lady!"

The Duck Boot Lady was named Sharon and she lived with her daughter. I can only speculate that they had a tempestuous relationship, which contributed to the angry expression on her face when I saw her every morning. She was in her early fifties and the daughter in her midthirties. The daughter left New Jersey after that Halloween and the hurricane and checked herself into a mental health clinic in Pennsylvania around the time we stopped seeing The Duck Boot Woman.

On Halloween night of that year, her daughter murdered her with a pickaxe. That was the reason she was not in line with me those days following the hurricane or any day after. The picture on the R.I.P. poster looked nothing like the agitated woman I stood next to every morning up until that November. No glasses, no scowl. A wide-eyed woman with a wide smile and optimistic eyes. I never picked up Sharon's route in Ewing but got one closer to home. A combination of complaints and the failing car led to an end of my courier career. I no longer see my friends from the morning and hope they are well and never suffer the fate of the woman I stood with every morning, who was murdered by her own daughter, and I never looked at a pair of webbed boots the same way since.

INSIDE A DANGEROUS MIND

Let me speak of worn-out worry, with idle time comes a flurry

Storming out the cerebellum of the dangerous mind of a potential felon

Combine the chaos and the terror that makes them see demons in the mirror

Add in antidepressants that just make things worse, this maniac's about to burst!

Then what you get my cautioned reader,

Is the shape that stalks in your nightmares, long kicks down longer flights of stairs

The boogeyman that's all too real, that shiver up your spine you feel

The killer in your closet door, contractors dumping bodies out to shore

The rent a clown that makes you cringe. Perhaps some heroin for that syringe?

Here's the backwoods local that gives terrible directions

The greasy haired pervert you unknowingly give erections

Inside your head they've all taken up residence

They're here with you in your residence and they have no interest in your dead presidents

They wish to kill and then kill again, may keep your corpse if they need a friend.

Stab it or fuck it? What shall they do? Some may devour and digest what once was you.

Even if you are not alone some dangerous minds can be prone

To access you through your loved ones, they too have mothers, daughters and sons.

They may maul a friend or decapitate a lover one of these psychos can be your own mother

Is that you Misses Bates at the motel off the interstate?

Checked in late poor desperate fools somehow drowned in that pool.

I was not there sir. I do not know. I took a mental vacay down in Mexico.

My passport's stamped. I'm not lying feel free to search my dangerous mind.

F13

Come dance with me under pale moonlight

Embrace the darkness terror and fright

Tomorrow's not promised just live for today

For on Friday the thirteenth, it can all go away

Stock Markets crash and vehicles smash into one another

Better check upstairs today I believe sisters killed brother

Today floor boards creak just a little bit louder

Today may put maggots in your salad or chowder

Damnation surrounds us all on this here day

Reschedule the flight good advice I'd say

That next vacation may be a final destination

As you descend to the ocean still alive on arrival

Swim with the sharks with no hope for survival

Sleep with the fishes ignore wise intuition.

Strangers may kill you just because you are home

Strangers phone babysitter from inside the home

Black cats are pouncing into nurseries possessed

To silence that baby and draw out its last breath

Madmen are howling from their diseased minds!

It's Friday the thirteenth! Redrum this sow is mine!

Legend BS and superstition the know it all say

Yet, mothers with child in womb tucked away

Wish not to give birth. No. Not on this day.

Little piggies shall squeal and run fast away

It's Friday the thirteenth and the Wolf's here to play

Doors open themselves in narrow hallways

Baby Judas was born? Well, you don't say!

Try not to suffer this day's your last supper

Ms. Leeds thirteenth child is here, he's your thirteenth guest

Sit beside the sinister over here to my left

That Amityville winds blowing into your house

It's Friday the thirteenth and you should *get out*!

And dance with the darkness of those who still Shine

Who were forged by the fire under moonlight divine

COMPLIMENTS OF CONTEMPT (FROM THAT TIME I DIED)

Remember, remember the thirteenth of November 2008, was it not great?!

That overcast morning we laid out fluids pouring

Remember the wreckage, smoke, and the rubble

Recall stupid questions as we bled out in trouble

Behind the car's wheel was my fault of course

Yet something kept me from staying the course

Yessir indeed, I'd be quite remiss

Should I forget my antagonists

For I may be guilty, but I'm not alone

I shan't forget you. Not in this poem.

I curse all of you, all wives, and all mothers

Stepfathers, sisters, aunties, and brothers

May your limbs twist in contortion,

All future heirs & wombs be abortioned

Choke on air and vomit water each day of your life

May an entity come and face-fuck you each night

Live in eternal misery, waterboarded by tears

See my bloody skull when passing a mirror

The day you marked me you brought upon this

A dish that's so cold, I shall feast upon it.

Flesh boils in hellfire souls roast in embers

Misfortune snap't bones and ruptured organs still remember

No we shall not forget you, nor the thirteenth of November

NIGHT O' THE KRAMPUS

L et's take a moment from holiday joy

Let's put aside good girls and good boys

Forget your goofy sweater party, and stall all the antics

It's December the fifth, and it's the night of the Krampus

Revisit the legend many knew all too well

Of the holiday demon derived out of hell

Forged in inferno by the dark one himself

Slaughtering reindeer and murdering elf

Burning down toy stores inspired by greed

Causing Radio Flyer sleds to smash into trees

What are those hooves plodding in crisp night air?

What is it that makes all wicked children despair?

What beats them, whips them? What rips out their hair?

With razor sharp teeth and the face of a beast

Growling and snarling this night on this day

The Krampus is here to take you away

Traveled from the darkest end of the North Pole

To rip open little brats' flesh and feed on their soul

It's a December disaster for little bitches and bastards

All year long you cried, pouted, whined, and griped

Summoning the Krampus who takes you this night

What are those hooves plodding in December night air?

What is it that makes all wicked children disappear?

TERROR REMAINS

All the spiders have left the walls. Cobwebs in the shrubs have all dissolved.

Killer Clowns are no longer hanging. Mummified Skeletons are no longer dangling.

Jack O' Lantern is now Pumpkin Pie. Ravens have left the Scarecrow's side.

Black Wreaths and Black Mirrors are packed away. Off the beaten path my Black Cat hath strayed.

The Undead have halted their ghastly march. No Harvest Moon lights up the dark.

Yet Evil remains in the still beating heart. Madmen that want to rip your limbs apart.

Lurking and stalking your every turn. Lunatics that just want to watch the world burn.

Wicked schemers still plotting to disrupt. Diseased minds boil over about to erupt.

How safe are you really in the present day? In a flash or an instant, it can all go away.

The fragile society would so quickly unravel a crumbling mess of burnt ash, rubble and gravel.

Survivors shall encounter much rabble in their travels through the desolate wasteland.

Every man woman and child living from mouth to the hand.

Dark Ages and Depressions we've lived through them sure.

Diseased rats bringing plague from ships to your shore.

Markets may crash even worse than before.

Diversify your portfolio, why bother? What for?

Tomorrow's not promised, that much I can promise

Dictators with buttons far too eager to touch. A code and a button it wouldn't take much.

A mushroom cloud in a November Sky? A hell of a topping for that Thanksgiving Pie.

No I'm not crazy, cynical, or insane I just understand terror

I understand it remains. Happy Thanksgiving

MAD NO MORE

A day you figured, should never come

Emerges steadfast, on your horizon

The madcap that you tried to numb

Holds the high card and he's smiling

Hands have been dealt

All bets laid down are final

Horrific torment shall be felt

Ablating cerebral down to spinal

Vicious whips you once wielded

Are bound so tight around your neck

For the madcap has the high card

Somehow he drew it from the deck

Pleased to overplay, your part

Shuffling him, in disregard

It's going to hurt like holy hell

Once he lays down that card

Content to have him pick up fifty-two

Forever stacking odds against

A madcap mad dog comes for you

He's chewed right through the fence

The pendulums prepped to penetrate

There shall be no Vaseline

As she puts it down, he eviscerates

All jacks, kings and their queens

Jokers in juries are hung

Hearts bled out, by spades

Diamonds smashed to bits, by clubs

A fitting end to your charade

Your games are at an end

The madcaps have just begun

In his sleeves aces slide back in

Should another like you come

The madcap played the high card

Dark victory? Damn straight! Damn sure!

Laughing last, but laughing hard

For what made him mad exists no more

ABOUT THE AUTHOR

Jason Marinko is an actor, author, and storyteller residing in New Jersey with his wonderfully loving and supportive girlfriend Michelle and his thumbless cowriters, Mister Speedy and Miss Selina Catface. He is graciously influenced by family, friends, and the amazing and interesting people he's been so fortunate to encounter along the way. Chance has bestowed upon him the greatest group of lifelong friends any individual could have as well as support from countless others that have made this and other works possible. The utmost thanks and appreciation to you all.

Everyone with me is family, and everybody's got me.
—Makavelli